"Look," Fargo said, "let's cut the cackle. I got a red-hot twirling chiquita waiting for me in Saint Joe. You want my services or don't you?"

Lattimer gave it some final thought. "All right, so you've set your sights on something bigger than three squares and a flop? Everybody knows you've depopulated half the West, but always in fair fights. But, see, a killer ain't necessarily a murderer, and my riders are all murderers—we don't leave no witnesses. How do I know you got the stones to burn a man down in cold blood?"

Quicker than eyesight Fargo's walnut-grip Colt leaped into his fist. He thumb-cocked it and leveled it toward Dog Man and Parsons.

"Jack's right—no need for a four-way split. Pick out the man I'm replacing, Mr. Lattimer, and I'll send him to hunt with the white buffalo."

THE TRAILSMAN

#372

MISSOURI MASTERMIND

by

Jon Sharpe

A SIGNET BOOK

SIGNET
Published by New American Library, a division of
Penguin Group (USA) Inc., 375 Hudson Street,
New York, New York 10014, USA
Penguin Group (Canada), 90 Eglinton Avenue East, Suite 700, Toronto,
Ontario M4P 2Y3, Canada (a division of Pearson Penguin Canada Inc.)
Penguin Books Ltd., 80 Strand, London WC2R 0RL, England
Penguin Ireland, 25 St. Stephen's Green, Dublin 2,
Ireland (a division of Penguin Books Ltd.)
Penguin Group (Australia), 250 Camberwell Road, Camberwell, Victoria 3124,
Australia (a division of Pearson Australia Group Pty. Ltd.)
Penguin Books India Pvt. Ltd., 11 Community Centre, Panchsheel Park,
New Delhi - 110 017, India
Penguin Group (NZ), 67 Apollo Drive, Rosedale, Auckland 0632,
New Zealand (a division of Pearson New Zealand Ltd.)
Penguin Books (South Africa) (Pty.) Ltd., 24 Sturdee Avenue,
Rosebank, Johannesburg 2196, South Africa

Penguin Books Ltd., Registered Offices:
80 Strand, London WC2R 0RL, England

First published by Signet, an imprint of New American Library,
a division of Penguin Group (USA) Inc.

First Printing, October 2012
10 9 8 7 6 5 4 3 2 1

The first chapter of this book previously appeared in *California Killers*, the three
hundred seventy-first volume in this series.

ALWAYS LEARNING   PEARSON

The Trailsman

Beginnings . . . they bend the tree and they mark the man. Skye Fargo was born when he was eighteen. Terror was his midwife, vengeance his first cry. Killing spawned Skye Fargo, ruthless, cold-blooded murder. Out of the acrid smoke of gunpowder still hanging in the air, he rose, cried out a promise never forgotten.

The Trailsman they began to call him all across the West: searcher, scout, hunter, the man who could see where others only looked, his skills for hire but not his soul, the man who lived each day to the fullest, yet trailed each tomorrow. Skye Fargo, the Trailsman, the seeker who could take the wildness of a land and the wanting of a woman and make them his own.

Saint Joseph, Northwest Missouri, 1861—where Skye Fargo discovers that beguiling beauty disguises unspeakable treachery.

1

"Fargo, I won't swallow your bunk like all them weak-sister inkslingers do," announced Jude Lattimer, squatting on his rowels to warm his hands over the sawing flames of a small campfire. "You come belly-crawlin' into our camp and actually b'lieve I'll just let you butt your saddle and leave this place alive? Old son, you're a bigger fool than God made you."

Skye Fargo knew he was dancing with death just by being here. Lattimer and his minions had camped on a bench of lush grass a stone's throw from the Missouri River, well hidden by a dense pine thicket. And clearly they didn't cotton to being discovered.

The man staring at him with dead bone chip eyes was capable of the instant brutality of a Comanche. And the two lunatic hyenas siding him were already measuring Fargo for a nameless grave.

"I walked in," Fargo reminded him evenly. "And I'm not one to peddle bunk. You can at least hear me out."

Lattimer picked at his teeth with a horseshoe nail, his unblinking eyes never once leaving Fargo's storied gun hand. He was a big, rawboned, hatchet-faced man with a livid white scar running from his left ear to the point of his jaw the legacy of a Cherokee war hatchet.

"I'll admit to being a mite curious," Lattimer said in a voice rough as corn shucks. "Ain't every day a *living legend* hails my camp. Speak your piece."

"I want to join up with you boys," Fargo announced without preamble.

Fargo's unexpected words stiffened all three men like hounds alerting. Their faces were brassy, hard-edged and hostile in the flickering light, cast partly in sinister shadow by their hat brims.

"The hell's your drift, Fargo?" Lattimer demanded. "Join up for what? We ain't startin' a club for crusading cockchafers."

"I know what you boys been up to," Fargo said. "And I'm offering my services—for the right price."

The man seated on a dead log to Lattimer's right reacted to Fargo's blunt words as if they were hard slaps. Fargo recognized him as Jack Parsons, a deep-chested, hulking brute with a drooping teamster's mustache and a face carved from granite. He rose slowly to his feet.

"Fargo," he said in a tone laced with menace, "every mother's son 'tween here and hell knows who and what you are. Yet, you got the oysters to tell us—"

"Sew up your lips, Jack," Lattimer snapped. "Your mouth runs like a whip-poor-will's ass—you know that? Plank your butt back down on that log."

Lattimer's bone-button eyes swiveled back to Fargo. "You got us crossed up with some other hombres, long-shanks. Join up? Hell, we're just three farmers down on our luck. Grasshoppers ate us off our land down near Sedalia."

"Farmers don't wear tie-down guns with the sights filed off," Fargo replied in his mild way. "You can cut the swamp gas. You three boys are behind the express robberies in this area—I know because I'm the best damn tracker in the West, and I followed your trail here from that heist on County Road."

Parsons's right hand inched toward his holster.

"Try it," Fargo said in a bored voice, "and you'll fry everlasting, Jack. Hell ain't *half* full."

"Look-a-here, Fargo," Lattimer said. "Let's just suppose you was right about us, which you ain't. Why would a famous son of a bitch like you want to hit the owlhoot trail all of a sudden like? It ain't your natural gait."

"Fame? Add fame to a nail, Lattimer, and you'll have a nail. Sure, being a newspaper 'hero' brings me a ration of cunny, but fame won't spend. I've had my bellyful of hardtack and wagon-yard whiskey, and I'm fed up with four-bit flophouses."

"He's a shit-eatin' liar!" Parsons spat out. "He's some sorta jackleg law dog, Jude! Sure, he's all togged out in buckskins like a mountain man, but he's drawing wages from the army or that lard-ass U.S. marshal in K.C. I say let's burn him down!"

Fargo's eyes narrowed to slits. "Jack, I rode in to parley with Mr. Lattimer. But if you're feeling froggy, go right ahead and jump."

Parsons eyed the tall, broad-shouldered Trailsman and realized he had no more fear in him than a rifle. He spat into the fire and clammed up.

This prodded a snort out of the third man present, who sat on a tree stump sharpening the twelve-inch blade of a bowie knife with a whetstone. A sawed-off twelve-gauge leaned against his left leg like a favorite pet, and his crossed bandoliers bristled with shells for it. He had a cauliflower ear from years of hard brawling.

Fargo had recognized him after a few minutes in camp: Willy "Dog Man" Lee, half-breed whelp of a Louisiana whore and a Cheyenne Dog Soldier.

"Don't pay no never-mind to Jack," Dog Man told Fargo. "He's what they call excitable—one of his *feminine* traits."

Lattimer ignored all this, still watching Fargo as if he were a bit of curiosa in a freak show. "So it's no more hog and hominy for you, huh? Do you ever take the time to smell what you're shoveling?"

"Straight-arrow, I want to throw in with you boys. If I was the law, why take this chance? I'd've just come in a-smokin'."

Lattimer mulled that. "But they say you're some pumpkins at a poker table. A man with good pasteboard skills can get on real good in Saint Joe."

"You don't win big unless you bet big. Mostly I can only afford joker poker for bungtown coppers and hard-times tokens. You can't salt away a decent stake by pounding your testicles against a saddle all your life, wet-nursing soldier blue. Two dollars a day while red aborigines try to turn my guts into tepee ropes."

"Stuff!" Parsons snarled. "Jude, he's lying through them pretty teeth of his. Skye Fargo ain't the kind—"

"I told you to put a stopper on your gob," Lattimer cut his lackey off. "Dog Man, do you know this hombre?"

"Well, he don't exactly stand in thick with me, Jude, but I know him, sure. I watched him knock the pie-biters outta some struttin' peacock lawman in Fort Griffin, Texas."

"A star-packer, you say?"

Dog Man nodded once, still working the bowie's blade. "Near 'bout killed him, too. Fargo knocked him into the middle of next week with a haymaker. I won ten simoleons on that dustup."

"Hunh."

Lattimer, eyes never leaving Fargo, slid his smoker's bible from a fob pocket, crimped a paper, and shook tobacco into it from a bull's-scrotum pouch on his belt. He quirled the ends expertly and lit a match on his tooth, fighting the wind for a light.

"Fargo," he said, "nobody ever said you ain't got sand. I just ain't so sure you could ever go crooked. Pounding a lawman into paste ain't the same as papering the walls with his brains. You got the *cojones* to *kill* a starman?"

"Deal me in and find out."

Lattimer smoked in silence, rubbing the scruff on his chin and conning it over. "Well, *if* I was who you say I am, it might be handy at that—having a by-God tracker who can use the stars at night and read bent grass and such. Handy as a pocket in a shirt."

Parsons heaved his big bulk to his feet again. "Jude, who's talkin' too much now?"

"Simmer down. We ain't pulling the wool over Fargo. Like he said, if he was the law, why show himself? He coulda plugged all three of us quicker 'n a finger snap."

"Jude's right about us needing a tracker, too," Dog Man chimed in. "Best time to shake a hemp committee is at night, and we've had considerable trouble in that regard. The outlaw trail takes some hellacious turns."

Parsons had cooled off some, but he was still stubbornly resistant. "I'm dead set against it. All right, so he's a tracker—"

"Not *a* tracker, chumley," Dog Man corrected him. "The best. He learned his lore from men you've only heard of."

"So what? That makes it a four-way split at our end, and we already hafta give up too much of the swag to that—"

"Pipe down, you chucklehead." Lattimer cut him off. "Nix on sayin' any damn names. Your tongue swings way too loose."

Parsons spat into the fire again. "Well, anyhow, I don't trust this bearded buckaroo. Hell, dame rumor has it that Pinkerton is in Saint Joe now. Maybe buckskin boy here is one a them 'eyes that never sleep.'"

"There's a joker in every deck," Fargo said calmly.

Dog Man snorted. "Ol' Jack here, he's got what you might call a hair-trigger contempt for famous men like you, Fargo."

"Christ," Fargo said. "I'm a broken man."

Lattimer and Dog Man snickered at this while Parsons tried to stare down the new arrival.

"Well, Jack ain't been bashful on *his* opinion," Lattimer said. "Dog Man?"

Hard-glinting eyes quick as a lasso sized up Fargo. "He looks about half rough, all right," the breed decided. "I'd poke into it a little more, but might be he'll do to take along."

"You two stupid galoots will be sorry," Parsons opined, washing his hands of it.

"You got to unnerstan'," Lattimer told Fargo. "Once you pitch into our game, you're on the dodge forever. The rest of your born days your back's to a wall, and every time a twig snaps, you'll jump like a butt-shot dog. You think you can stomach that?"

"Hell," Fargo said, "I live that way now. Seems like every swinging dick on the frontier is notching his sights on me. I might's well pocket some color for all that risk."

"You wanna talk color?" Lattimer said. "Just a whoop and a holler from here sits the keys to the mint, Trailsman. A big transport safe full of gold bullion."

"That's a sight of money," Fargo agreed.

"A *damn* sight though the pie has to be sliced more than four ways. But it ain't just law dogs and shotgun riders we got to fret. This area is lousy with jayhawker gangs and border ruffians—plenty of 'em learned easy-go killing down in the Mexer war, and they're no boys to fool with. That lever-action long gun a yours won't stay in the scabbard long, I guarandamntee it."

5

"Look," Fargo said, "let's cut the cackle. I got a red-hot twirling chiquita waiting for me in Saint Joe. You want my services or don't you?"

Lattimer gave it some final thought. "All right, so you've set your sights on something bigger than three squares and a flop? Everybody knows you've depopulated half the West, but always in fair fights. But, see, a killer ain't necessarily a murderer, and my riders are all murderers—we don't leave no witnesses. How do I know you got the stones to burn a man down in cold blood?"

Quicker than eyesight Fargo's walnut-grip Colt leaped into his fist. He thumb-cocked it and leveled it toward Dog Man and Parsons.

"Jack's right—no need for a four-way split. Pick out the man I'm replacing, Mr. Lattimer, and I'll send him to hunt with the white buffalo."

2

Fargo's unexpected announcement shocked all three men into a motionless silence. He wagged the barrel of his Colt.

"Pick one, Lattimer," he repeated. "I hope it's Parsons. I think his boots will fit me."

"Now, Fargo, just hold your horses," Parsons said, his voice reedy with fright. "Jude, tell this crazy son of a bitch to leather that shooter."

"Katy Christ," Dog Man said. "Did you *magic* that gun into your hand?"

Lattimer suddenly emitted a harsh bark of laughter. "Shit, Fargo, are you serious?"

Fargo grinned and twirled his gun into his holster. "Nah. I don't need work *that* bad. But I will plug any man, woman, child or mule you tell me to. I ride for the brand, and you're the big he-bear in this den."

"Well, by God, I like your style. Consider yourself hired."

"Essence of lockjaw?" Dog Man asked, offering Fargo a bottle of whiskey that glowed a lurid red in the flames. The Trailsman knocked back a slug, feeling it burn in a straight line to his gut and make his nostrils sting.

"*There's* medicine," he said, passing the bottle to Parsons, who looked like he needed it.

"Fargo," Lattimer said, "here's what I don't quite savvy. You don't know me. We ain't never met. Matter fact, I never even laid eyes on you before you sneaked up on us. Since I make it a point to avoid a reputation, how do you even know about me?"

"That's easy," Fargo said. "I fucked your sister."

There was another long, shocked silence while the fire

7

crackled and the cicadas droned ceaselessly. Lattimer's inscrutable mask cracked, and for a few moments he looked like a man who had woken in the wrong century. He pulled the cigarette from his mouth and blinked stupidly. "You what?"

"I don't believe I spoke Choctaw. 'Bout a year ago down in Arkansas, I pounded the spike maul to Charlene while that dumb yack she's married to was driving hogs into Progress City."

"Christ, Fargo. You don't just up and tell a man you screwed his sister."

"You asked how I knew about you. I wasn't looking to offend you."

"Hell, I don't take no offense. I poked her a few times myself after she growed some tits on her."

All this was too much for Dog Man and Parsons, who ended up rolling on the ground and howling with mirth.

"Say, boss," Parsons sputtered between paroxysms of laughter, "I guess that sorter makes you and Fargo kin, huh?"

"'At's right," Dog Man managed to chime in. "Sounds like ol' Charlene was *ate* before she was seven."

Lattimer's head swiveled slowly in their direction. "If you two gazabos are lookin' for your own graves, I'll help you find 'em. Wipe them grins off your dials."

"Anyhow," Fargo said, "she was proud as a peacock about you. Said you could outshoot and outfight any hard case in the country. Showed me a tintype of you, too, and I recognized you right off tonight from the scar."

"She flaps her jaws too much, just like these two knotheads. Well, I reckon your chiquita is waiting to climb all over you in town. You staying in Saint Joe?"

Fargo shook his head. "I been bedding down in the woods. I'm a mite light in the pockets."

Lattimer nodded and pulled a gold shiner from a hip pocket, flipping it to Fargo. He could tell instantly, from the heft of it when he caught it, that it was a double eagle.

"Twenty dollars," Fargo said, whistling. "Wish *I* had a farm go bust."

"There's a livery just two streets behind the old Pony Express stables," Lattimer said. "A cantankerous old rooster named Septimus Perkins runs it. He'll take good care of your horse, and let you spread your blankets in an empty stall, for eight bits a night. Hole up there for a few days. I'll get word to you."

"Sounds jake to me," Fargo said, pocketing the shiner. "Thanks for the stake."

"That's small potatoes compared to what you stand to make. But I'll give it to you with the bark still on it—us three ain't the whole kit 'n' caboodle. We're part of what you might call a syndicate. There's more in town, and you'll be watched. You try to put handles on us and turn us around, mister, and you'll wish you'd died as a child."

Fargo rode back to his rustic camp about a mile upstream, eyes in constant motion in the silvery moon wash. He didn't need Lattimer to convince him that Missouri, in the 1860s, was hard ground. Desperate, lawless elements had plunged the state into chaos, and the only safety was in numbers— well-armed numbers. A lone rider was likely to be shot for his tobacco.

"Well, old campaigner," he muttered to the Ovaro, "we jumped over a snake that time. But the shitstorm is still ahead of us."

They reached the pine thicket, hidden by a tangled dead-fall, where Fargo had slept the last two nights. He swung down and stripped the stallion down to the neck leather, then let him tank up from a little rill nearby. Fargo put him on a short ground tether and gave him a quick rub with an old feed sack.

Graze was lush along the river, but Fargo wasn't about to let a fine horse like this stay exposed in bright moonlight. He poured the last crushed barley into his hat from a gunny sack tied to his saddle horn and grained his horse.

The Ovaro snuffled indignantly when the scant rations were gone, shoving his nose into Fargo's chest hard in protest.

"You'll eat good tomorrow," Fargo promised. "Both of us will."

Fargo slid his 16-shot Henry from its scabbard and propped it against a tree next to the fire pit he had dug. He pulled a handful of crumbled bark from a saddle pocket and tossed it into the pit for kindling. The early-spring night was raw with chill, but soon he had a small, Apache-style "personal fire" crackling, just enough heat to warm his hands and face if he leaned close.

Fargo gnawed on a tasteless hunk of salt junk while he ran the events of this night through his mind. Usually it was his way to wade in slowly, testing the waters. But tonight he had plunged in headlong, reckless and harum-scarum, and his fate was far from assured.

Jack Parsons—an excellent express-safe cracksman and a fair gunhand—was hotheaded and predictable. But Lattimer and Dog Man were cool, ruthless and cunning, and Fargo knew his life was forfeit if he was fool enough to trust them. Lattimer might well have sent him to Perkins's livery so he'd know exactly where to kill him.

"Pile on the agony," Fargo muttered as he rolled up in his blanket and stretched back with his head on his saddle.

The wind soughed in the pine boughs, lulling him toward sleep, and the wide Missouri flowed past with a steady, peaceful chuckle. A star-shot sky and the singsong of frogs and crickets reminded Fargo why he hated to sleep under a roof.

But just before he tumbled over the threshold of sleep, Fargo heard a new noise added to the night chorus—the rapid ticking of wood-burrowing insects. The fine hairs on his nape stiffened.

The insects were popularly known as deathwatch beetles. And according to backcountry lore, they were only heard before somebody died.

"Say, mister!"

Fargo hauled back on the reins as a slope-shouldered, wreath-bearded pilgrim dressed in gray homespun hurried toward him.

"Mister, you appear to be a frontiersman," he greeted Fargo. "Am I correct in that surmise?"

It was only an hour after sunup, but already the muddy, wagon-rutted streets of Saint Joe were writhing with activity. The settlement, built on a bulge of land formed by a sharp bend in the Missouri, was one of the "big jump-offs" to the Wild West. Steamboats arrived every day, holds and decks chockablock with cattle, chicken coops, plows, washtubs, furniture—and the hopeful, nervous faces of the great westward migration.

One of those faces stared up at Fargo now, praying for the right answer.

"I do spend most of my time out beyond the settlements, friend," Fargo replied, guessing what was coming.

"Sir, I represent a group of two hundred souls from Bucks County, Pennsylvania. We—"

"You had a contract with a conductor who promised to guide you to Oregon," Fargo finished for him. "You folks took up a collection and paid him half in advance. And now you can't find hide nor hair of him."

The pilgrim nodded, too desperate to look ashamed. "Now we're marooned. Would you be interested in serving as our guide? We'll pay what we can."

Fargo felt a pang behind his heart. These beleaguered tenderfoots had a dream swelling inside them—a dream that somewhere in the great beyond was a perfect piece of land that meant security and fulfillment. That great need made them perfect targets for every manner of ruthless swindler.

"It's not in my line," Fargo replied, not unkindly, as he leaned forward against the saddle horn. "And even if it was, I've got other irons in the fire."

The man's face sagged into a mask of hopeless despair.

"Listen," Fargo said. "There's a tavern on Center Street called the Mayflower. The bar dog is a big Irishman named Red Mike. He's straight goods. Go see him. Tell him a bearded jasper riding an Ovaro sent you. He'll set you folks up with an honest conductor. You have my cast-iron guarantee you won't regret it."

The desperate emigrant looked up into the crop-bearded, weather-bronzed face with its direct, lake blue eyes that seemed focused on the far distances. He nodded, hope surging into his face.

"I sure will, mister. I *sure* will! Thank you!"

Fargo touched his hat and gigged the Ovaro forward. Mercantile stores, gun shops, wheelwrights and blacksmiths abounded, all doing a lively trade at this time of year, the air crisp with spring weather and the lure of the Great Unknown.

Fargo knew the westering fever would not likely surpass the fiddle-footed '50s, but even this late the boom was still on.

The streets were already thronged with pedestrian and animal traffic. On a grassy sward on the bluffs north of town, new and refitted wagons were halted tongue to tail as the westering companies formed in an atmosphere of constant excitement and activity. The excitement would tail off, Fargo knew, as these back-easters discovered the number of graves along the Oregon Trail—as many as seventeen per mile by Fargo's count.

Won't be too long, he thought morosely, and the entire West will be peopled up. And innocent pilgrims aside, plenty of the men flocking to the frontier would shame the devil in hell.

That thought made him cast a wary eye all about him. He recalled Lattimer's warning from last night: *We're part of what you might call a syndicate. There's more in town, and you'll be watched.*

Rains had been heavy lately and the street was a spongy quagmire. But most of the merchants, in a gesture to the many women and children, had laid duckboards down to facilitate walking. A Choctaw from the Nations, wrapped in muddied scarlet strouding, lay dead drunk—or perhaps just dead—in the middle of the street, an impervious island around which the stream of traffic divided.

Fargo rode past the elegant and famous Patee House, the finest hotel west of the Mississippi, and cut right for two blocks, veering into the hoof-packed yard of a big, ramshackle livery barn. He lit down and led the Ovaro inside by the bridle reins.

"Hey-up!" he called into the manure-fragrant dimness. "I'm looking for Septimus Perkins."

"Look for a cat's tail!" groused a gravel-pitted voice from the shadowy interior. "Hell, the day's still a pup! Let an old man sleep, why'n'cha?"

"Stir your stumps, old-timer. I got a hungry stallion here that needs oats and a currycomb."

"This ain't the only feed stable in town, mister. Le'me sleep."

"Can't, Dad." Fargo slipped the bit and the cinch. "I got places to go and people to meet. Roust out!"

Fargo grinned at the string of hot curses. A small, thin, flat-chested old man wearing red long-handles and a straw Chihuahua hat materialized out of the dimness, straw still clinging to him.

"Easy for you young bucks to be piss and vinegar this early," he complained. "My age, it takes a while to get up a head of steam."

Fargo took in the slat-ribbed elder's craggy face and lumpish chin. He walked on unsteady sea legs and smelled like a mash vat. Fargo recognized the type instantly: Advancing age had forced him to seek civilization, but even the most rustic outpost was too civilized for him. A true curmudgeon who found it too onerous to perform the meeting rituals. A type Fargo admired.

"Looks like you cut the wolf loose last night," Fargo remarked.

"Bo, I was out on the roof, for a surety. My tongue feels like a cat turd rolled in cracker crumbs."

The old codger's bleary eyes had just focused on Fargo's black-and-white horse. "Say! That's one humdinger of a stallion."

"He ain't the worst old nag," Fargo said, and the Ovaro lashed him in the face with his tail. "You must be Septimus?"

"Ain't like I got a choice."

Now Septimus turned his attention to the tall, buckskin-clad stranger, narrowing his eyes. "I ain't met too many white men what don't cut their horses."

"I like spirit in a horse. How much spirit would *you* have if somebody lopped off your nuts?"

"Wouldn't hardly matter, bo. My fires was banked long ago. Hell, I ain't even piss-proud in the morning."

Fargo thumbed his hat back and looked around. His eyes had adjusted to the dimness, and he found himself in a surprisingly tidy and clean livery barn. Perhaps ten horses were presently stalled, all well groomed and appearing content.

"I didn't catch your name," the hostler said.

"I didn't toss it."

"Huh. Likely it would just be a summer name anyhow. I'll just call you Buckskins."

13

"This is the frontier, old roadster. You don't nose a man's backtrail."

"Used to, I never did. But it ain't just green-antlered pilgrims filling Saint Joe, Buckskins. Three times now I been heisted. The last son of a bitch conked me on the cabeza so hard my ears was squirtin' blood."

Fargo tossed his saddle onto a wooden rack and hung his bridle on a coffee can nailed to the wall. "Does this look like an outlaw horse to you?"

Septimus grunted. "A good point, and I'm caught upon it. This animal ain't been spurred a-tall."

"He's not mean, but let him get a good smell of you before you get too close—he's a biter."

"Sell your ass. I was breaking mustangs to leather down in the old Spanish land-grant country while you was still on ma's milk."

"I'm told eight bits a night includes a stall for me, too?"

Septimus nodded, yawning and digging at his left armpit. "But no Eastern money. I'll take gold or silver only."

"Sounds jake to me. I'll square with you after I eat breakfast and run some errands."

"Funny," Septimus said, watching Fargo as he slid his Henry from the scabbard. "You don't look like no errand boy to me. Matter fact, Buckskins, you look like a man what's done a fair share of killing in his day."

"Kill one fly," Fargo said as he headed through the wide doors, "kill a million."

3

Fargo hadn't seen Saint Joe since it replaced Independence as the favorite gateway to the West, and the yondering loner in him detested the jostling crowds and filthy streets choked with garbage, dead animals and human night soil. He spotted a hog reeve driving several rooting pigs off the rammed-earth sidewalks.

It was the two-legged animals, however, that occupied his attention. All the capital changing hands drew unsavory elements, and hard-bitten men lounging against buildings watched him from hooded glances. Any one of them, he reminded himself, could be part of the "syndicate" Jude Lattimer had alluded to.

Fargo walked two blocks toward the river and reached a pine-log establishment whose gilt-lettered window announced it as the Hog's Breath saloon. He shouldered the batwings and entered a dark and smoky interior that reeked of tobacco and lye soap.

He glanced around, noting that little had changed since he was last here. Despite the early hour, the long plank counter at the front was crowded with a motley assortment of men, most of them too busy conversing to pay much attention to one more stranger in a town growing rich from them.

"Skye Fargo, as I live and breathe!" a plump, pleasant, middle-aged woman in a dirty apron greeted him as he stepped up to one end of the counter. "Been a coon's age, long-tall."

"Good to see you again, Katy. Looks like the place is booming."

"Keeps me busier than a moth in a mitten. What brings a bunch-quitter like you to Saint Joe?"

"Just drifting through and decided to get outside of some hot grub. I'm so hungry my backbone is scraping against my ribs."

Katy leered suggestively. "Mm-hmm. You have a reputation for working up an appetite when you're in a town, Lothario. I'll have the Turk rustle you up some buckwheat cakes and side meat."

Fargo purchased beer and two boiled eggs and moved to a table in the far back corner, placing his back to a wall. He sat quietly munching the eggs and watching the flow of humanity through a large front window—and making sure no one had followed him inside.

When Fargo spotted her, he couldn't quite believe his eyes.

She was a pale blond beauty dressed regally in a cut-velvet suit and twirling a pongee parasol. She glanced through the glass and her eyes—ice blue—caught Fargo's admiring stare. He marveled at her finely sculpted cheekbones and fluid, sensuous lips that hinted she was a woman with a short sexual fuse.

Those tantalizing lips twitched for a moment, stopping just short of a smile, before she moved on.

"Good luck with *that* one, Trailsman," Katy said as she plunked a heaping platter of food down in front of him. "You're man enough for her, all right, but all *her* men can afford to keep a carriage."

"Maybe she dabbles in charity. Who is she?"

"Name's Inge Johanson. A Swedish culture vulture who's got an opera house planned for Saint Joe."

Fargo tied into his breakfast. "A society woman in Saint Joe?" he said skeptically. "All the pig shit would make a buzzard puke."

"There's some *very* rich men here, Skye, and her without a husband—yet. I expect she means to set herself up as our own Mrs. Astor."

"Interesting," Fargo said. "Any chance I could go down in the cellar when I finish this fine grub?"

Katy's eyes narrowed speculatively. "Oh *ho*! 'Just drifting through,' my sweet aunt. What can of worms are you opening this time?"

Fargo assumed a mien of cherubic innocence, but said nothing.

"'Course you can go down," she replied. "My lands, after the way you ran those Red Oak Boys out of here? Skye, they were bleeding me dry. I'll deny you nothing."

She made that last word resonate with layers of possibility before hurrying back to the counter. Fargo finished his meal and headed for a door midway along the nearest wall. Four dirt steps down took him into a damp storage cellar filled with beer barrels and crates of whiskey.

Fargo scratched a lucifer to life and rolled a barrel aside to lift a trap in the floor. When Saint Joe was still a fledgling settlement, Indian attacks had been numerous and "Indian tunnels" were common to escape danger. The settlement was too big and well armed for attacks now, with most of the area tribes driven south to the Indian Territory, and most of the tunnels were forgotten.

But Fargo needed to make sure that anyone waiting for him outside in the street would lose their quarry. If word got back to Lattimer and his cohorts about where Fargo was going, the Trailsman might soon be getting his mail delivered by moles.

Fargo had once used this low, dank tunnel to get the drop on the Red Oak Boys, a gang of thugs out of Arkansas who had plagued Saint Joe in the early 1850s. Now he followed it two streets over, making egress behind a stack of lumber in an alley between the new courthouse and Charles Street.

Eyes constantly scanning, Fargo headed for a small frame building at the corner of Charles and Tenth Streets. The only thing identifying the building as a place of business was a large eye over the door—the famous "eye that never sleeps."

"Ahh, here he is—the bearded, steely-eyed hero of the rapid-action whizbangs. Fargo, did you initiate contact?"

A nervous Allan Pinkerton fired the question at Fargo even before the latter had finished slacking into a chair in front of the detective's desk—a carved mahogany desk the size of west Texas. Pinkerton was a slightly paunchy man wearing bushy burnsides and a smoke gray wool suit, his manner brisk and businesslike. A Scottish brogue was evident in his trilled *r*'s and elongated vowels.

"Initiate contact?" Fargo repeated, hanging his hat on his left knee. "If that means did I palaver with Lattimer, yeah—last night."

The canny, neatly bearded sleuth's square face came alive with interest. "And did they accept your proposal?"

"I'd say I'm neither up the well nor down. Lattimer claims I'm in the gang, but he might just have said that to get shut of me."

"That's certainly possible. Tell me, did you really . . . intrigue with Lattimer's sister in Arkansas?"

"I 'intrigued' her several times, and I was smart to bring it up last night. Broke the ice, you might say. But they'll hash everything over in my absence, and if they decide it's too dicey, they'll have to kill me. Lattimer admitted they leave no witnesses."

Pinkerton nodded. "Well, dinna fash yourself, lad," he said in his trilling brogue. "If you weren't accepted, they'd have likely killed you on the spot."

"It's not like I was stupid enough to give them that chance. They know *I* know, and that might get me killed first chance they get to ambush me."

"If you believe the danger to yourself is too—"

"Hang the danger. For fifty dollars a week I'd ride into hell with a pocket full of firecrackers. I'm not a volunteer in this deal. *You* looked me up, remember?"

Pinkerton's broad brow wrinkled as he frowned. "Yes, God forgive me, because desperate situations call for desperate remedies. You're certainly effective, Fargo, as legions of dead criminals could testify. But your violent and heavy-handed methods won't work here. Modern scientific crime detection is far more effective than brute force in a case this intricate."

"I've noticed you talk like a book. Way I see it, if it pounds nails it's a hammer. Look here, there's something I don't savvy—if you already know that Lattimer and his greasy-sack outfit are pulling the heists, why'n't you just put the kibosh on them?"

Pinkerton shook his head in sad reproof. An 1861 calendar on the wall behind him advertised O. F. Winchester's new armaments factory.

"Fargo, there you go again. Guns blazing, kill every living thing you see. Lattimer and his minions can easily be replaced—it's the powers behind them we most want to sink."

"Hell, it's just one more express-robber gang, innit? More brutal than most, maybe, but—"

Pinkerton silenced him by raising one plump, pink-mottled hand. "You have grasped the obvious and missed the essence, my benighted operative. Fargo, do you stay abreast of financial matters?"

Fargo snorted. "I know when my pockets are empty. Why do you ask?"

"One thing I'm sure you do know is that, for many westering pioneers and adventurers, it all starts here in Saint Joseph. Only Virginia City, on the Comstock, has amassed more capital in need of transport."

Pinkerton had a flair for the dramatic and paused for effect. "Right now the U.S. Treasury is facing a serious monetary crisis. You've noticed, of course, how the government is *trying* to replace gold and silver coins with U.S. notes? So-called greenbacks? The trial is in its infancy and faring poorly."

Fargo nodded, recalling Septimus Perkins and his earlier refusal to accept such notes. "Most folks don't cotton to folding money, and neither do I. I want the value right there in my hand, not in some damn 'promissory note' from a bunch of swindlers in Washington City."

"Yes, but by next year, like it or not, the promissory note will be in wide circulation. You see, the government is trying to protect the country from gold hoarding. With paper they can keep the likes of Cornelius Vanderbilt from what amounts to taking over the country."

"The hell. They'll make cheese out of chalk before they ever stop the money grubbers and New York land hunters. Look how the federal government is kowtowing to the railroad barons."

Pinkerton expelled a fluming sigh of impatience. "Fargo, forget Sherwood Forest and your 'rugged individualism' for a moment. The point is that a new regulation is in the works— one that will not allow the Treasury to print any more paper money until the gold backing it is actually locked up in their vaults."

Despite his animosity Fargo was being drawn in as he saw where this trail was going.

"All these heists lately in Kansas and Missouri," Pinkerton resumed, "have drastically slowed down the stocking of paper issue. In fact, it's almost being brought to a screeching whoa, laddiebuck. If the paper-money plan fails, this great republic could someday be taken over by a gold-rich tyrant. It's happened before in Europe."

Fargo was indeed a bunch-quitter with little use for governments, but he grasped the importance of what Pinkerton had just said. America was still, politically speaking, an experiment in democratic freedom—an experiment that could still easily fail.

"The spirit of 'seventy-six," Pinkerton resumed, "could end up on the slag heap of history, defeated by the same monarchic despotism the founding fathers defeated."

"Yessir, you talk *just* like a book," Fargo said. "But I take your meaning. The government has hired you to make an example of the ring working in this region."

"Precisely. In fact, that's why I opened this new office in Saint Joseph. And you're the linchpin, Fargo. I've got two more operatives working this case full-time, along with myself. You, however, are the only one who has successfully infiltrated them."

"You're getting ahead of the roundup. I don't know that I'm in yet. You're sure this is an inside job?"

Pinkerton nodded gravely. "It has to be. In the three robberies so far, the secret routes—known only to the military and the express offices—were clearly no secret to the criminals. Only a fairly high-level employee of the express lines, a former employee or perhaps a high-ranking army officer could have known those routes. I don't believe, however, that the true head of the ring has anything to do directly with the actual holdups."

"You got any idea who the power behind the gang is?"

"Thanks to some excellent work by one of your fellow—perhaps I should say, *feminine*—operatives, it's been tentatively narrowed down to three suspects, all prominent citizens from this area."

"Feminine?" Fargo repeated, interest sparking in his eyes.

Pinkerton scowled. "Let's get one thing clear—I know your reputation for copulating with anything that moves."

"Motion isn't always required," Fargo said from a deadpan.

"Damn your impertinent bones, Fargo, I *mean* this— your relationship with your fellow operatives is to remain strictly professional at all times."

Now Fargo leaned forward, rapt with attention. "Say . . . this must be some fine dolly bird or you wouldn't be turning purple like that. S'matter—she wouldn't let you under her petticoats?"

"This unknown mastermind," Pinkerton said as if Fargo had never spoken, "runs his criminal empire without direct involvement. For now, I want you to solidify your position within Lattimer's little group and learn whatever you can. There will be a meeting soon, here in this office, at which you'll meet the other two operatives and be brought up to date."

Pinkerton banged open a desk drawer and handed Fargo a little bundle wrapped in soft leather.

"What's this?"

"A detective kit I have assembled for all my operatives. It will assist you in your investigations."

Trying not to smirk, Fargo opened the bundle and inspected the contents. There was a pocket-size "dark lantern," equipped with a sliding panel to block the light; a four-bitted "bar key" that would open most door locks of the day; a bar of soft wax to make impressions; handcuffs; a magnifying glass; and— truly amusing Fargo—a whistle to "stop fleeing felons" as Pinkerton gravely phrased it.

Pinkerton bristled when Fargo laughed outright at the tin whistle. "Remember, Fargo, the Pinkerton Agency does not condone 'flight law.' To you flight is absolute evidence of guilt; under the law, however, it is only *presumed conscious- ness* of guilt."

"These fleeing felons—should I also powder their butts and tuck them in at night?"

Pinkerton ignored the remark. "You're notorious for gun- fights, but I seriously doubt you've ever shot a man in the back."

"No," Fargo agreed with a straight face. "Generally I

21

shoot them in the leg and then kill them when they spin around."

Pinkerton gave him a baleful look. "I presume that was a joke?"

"It was," Fargo replied with equal solemnity. "But it spoils the fun if you have to ask."

Pinkerton hooked a thumb toward the door. "I'll let you know about the meeting. Now please vacate the premises before my dyspepsia acts up."

Fargo laughed and unfolded to his full six feet. "All right, old sobersides, I'm going. Just remember—*you* sent for me to help on this deal. I'll try to play this by your rules, but don't close-herd me. My ass is already hanging in the wind, and *this*"—Fargo waved the detective kit—"ain't worth a busted trace chain. Lead *will* fly, and when it does I won't be blowing any damn tin whistles."

4

A sneeze-bright sun was still low in the east when Fargo, after a careful reconnoiter of the street, slipped out of Pinkerton's office and hoofed it back to the livery. He stopped on Charles Street to watch a medicine-show juggler tossing a dizzying number of bright balls in a blurry circle. Fargo purchased a paper sack of gingersnaps from a vendor pushing a cart, but resumed his journey when an oily-looking "doctor" leaped onto a barrel and started hawking bottles of Dr. Holbrook's Scrofula and Piles Elixir.

About a block from the livery he literally ran smack into trouble.

Fargo had just rounded the corner when a drunken Jack Parsons, a fiery redhead on his arm, plowed into Fargo and sent him staggering. The Trailsman deftly kept his balance, but his gingersnaps were scattered in the muddy street.

"Sling your hook, you splayfooted bastard!" Parsons snarled. Then recognizing Fargo from the night before, his tone became grudgingly civil. "You're a mite clumsy, mister."

Fargo ignored him, his eyes raking over the redhead. Her flaming-copper hair, worn long and loose in back in the new "American style," was offset by emerald green eyes that seemed to mock and dare him at the same time. Her lips put him in mind of juicy berries ripe for the picking.

"Like what you see?" she challenged him in a purring voice that was almost as intimate as it was insouciant.

"I like it enough that I'd welcome seeing more," he replied frankly.

"Well, you're cocksure, are'n'cha?" She lightly emphasized the first syllable of "cocksure." "Also a mite whiffy. Hot baths only cost two bits."

"Would that include help scrubbing my back?"

Those ruby-fruit lips parted in amusement. "Well, now . . . *here's* a game one. Not one to mealymouth a gal, are you?"

"Faint heart never won fair lady."

Parsons scowled darkly. He'd had his bellyful of Fargo the night before. "Dust, hombre. You're the third button on a two-button shirt."

Fargo continued to ignore him, trying to puzzle this deal out. The woman had too many curves to brake for, creamy-lotion skin, and inviting eyes that taunted "come thrill me, knave." And evidently, she had a dangerous penchant for brutish, unshaven men who changed their names frequently. That didn't mesh with the expensive taffeta gown and fancy, side-lacing shoes with mother-of-pearl buttons.

Parsons grabbed her arm roughly. "Christ, why'n't you just set 'em on the glass for him? C'mon, I only got the room for an hour."

She tugged a six-inch pin from her hat and jabbed it into Parsons's brawny arm.

"*Owwch*, you little she-bitch! The hell you think—?"

"Kiss a chicken on the lips, Jacky boy," she said demurely, still sizing up the tall, buckskin-clad stranger with the inva-sive blue stare that tickled her secret parts. "I just might be looking at my next *amour fou*."

Parsons was still rubbing his arm. "The hell's that mean?"

"A crazy love," she informed him, still watching Fargo. "This bronzed stallion is a cut above."

"Piss on that trail bum, you little slut! You nagged me half-haywire to get us a room. Let's get thrashing."

"You'll have to forgive my randy companion, long-tall," she told Fargo. "He's eager to cut the buck loose."

"Can't say's I blame him, cupcake. You'd turn a gelding into a stud."

"I said step off!" Parsons snapped, doubling his ham-size fists and taking a menacing step toward Fargo. "You'd better check the brand before you drive another man's stock."

Fargo gave that the laugh it deserved. "And *you*, blow-hard, best learn to recognize a free-range maverick."

"I'm gonna cook your hash, mouthpiece," Parsons said,

eyes going smoky with rage. He tucked his chin and waded in, breath whistling in his nostrils.

Fargo had learned, from hard experience, never to let a raging bull get a death hug on him. He deftly sidestepped the charging hulk, throwing a looping blow to his jaw as he lunged harmlessly past.

He might just as well have slugged sacked salt. Parsons was too enraged to feel the blow. He caught himself, skidding hard, and pivoted fast toward Fargo. But this time the Trailsman used the attacker's own momentum against him, slamming him with a vicious uppercut that snapped Parsons's head back and dropped him on his ass hard in the street, still conscious but eyes glassy and unfocused.

Fargo would rather have avoided locking horns with Parsons just yet—this humiliation just now would hardly increase Fargo's chances of infiltrating the express-robber gang. But this feisty redhead *liked* to stir men up to combat over her, and he was damned if he was going to go puny on her before he got under her dainties.

The audible increase in her breathing proved he had excited her. "The name is Lily Reece," she told him. "And I'd just bet you're Skye Fargo—word's out that you just arrived in Saint Joe."

Fargo touched the brim of his hat. "Pleased."

"Likewise. It won't bother me if you keep me in mind," she told him, eyeing the Arkansas toothpick protruding from his boot.

"That's all right for starters, Lily. But a man can only get so far when he keeps a woman in his mind."

She tossed her head back and laughed, then brushed the tip of her tongue along her upper lip, those lucid green eyes promising him things. "Number seventeen Enterprise Street. I live with my father, but he's out every night until at least midnight."

Parsons shook his head, trying to hoist himself onto one knee.

"Best if you skedaddle, Mr. Fargo," she added. "Jacky Boy is strong as horseradish, but stupid and bullheaded. If you stay here you'll have to kill him. And then you'll owe the undertaker five dollars."

Fargo was town-broke and knew the rule in Missouri: If you killed it, you buried it. He touched his hat again and cast a wistful glance at his ruined gingersnaps before he strolled off, his sore right fist throbbing like an Apache war drum.

"Lily Reece?" Septimus Perkins repeated. He whistled sharply. "Un-unh, bo, give *that* little strumpet the go-by. She's naught but trouble."

Septimus was busy pounding caulks into old horseshoes. His skinny arms were blue-corded with veins. "Trouble," he repeated emphatically. "Oh, she'd make a dead man come, all right, but that fine little cunny of hers is the crack of doom, Buckskins."

"Trouble in a woman can add savor," Fargo replied.

"Ahuh. Well, my old peeder has turned to cheese, but iffen *I* was a young buck, I'd seek out a fence with a knothole in it afore I'd prong *that* little hellcat. She looks silky, sure, but she's a 'fast young woman' as the crapsheets say. Rumor has it she even likes to strip buck and take a buggy whip to her men afore they top her. Onliest way she can get het up."

"Hmm," was all Fargo said to that. "Who's her old man?"

"Who is Josiah Reece? Lad, where you been grazing? Christ, her pap is the goldang mayor of Saint Joe! Oh, the 'lection was crooked as cat shit, but they always are. He's the big bushway, all right."

That news rocked Fargo back on his heels. Why would the mayor's daughter—a breathtaking daughter, at that—be running around with hard criminal trash like Jack Parsons? Then again, there were times when Fargo actually preferred cheap whiskey.

Fargo was perched on the tongue of a big dray wagon in the livery yard, working his back teeth with a hog-bristle brush. He pulled it out and said, "Last time I drifted this way, a fire-and-brimstone preacher named Lansford Stratton was mayor."

"Ahuh, until somebody added lead to his diet. But Reece didn't have him killed—the stupid bastard tried to break up a gunfight by steppin' into the middle of it waving his Bible. He figured the Lord would protect him, I reckon, but he kallated wrong."

Septimus crossed to a barrel beside the stone water trough and pulled out a crockery jug. He tipped it back, liquor dribbling down his chin, and carried it over to Fargo.

"Have a snort to wash your teeth. It's potato whiskey— shit ain't too bad iffen you put your fist through a wall to help it down."

"No, thanks, old-timer. That homemade stuff will raise blood blisters on a new saddle. I'm one for a cold beer."

"Ahh, you young bucks nowadays and your damn barley pop. Say . . . strike a light! Now *here* comes a by-God female!"

Fargo followed the old man's gaze and spotted the same demure blonde who had stared at him through the window earlier. She was arm in arm with a balding, muttonchopped, middle-aged man dressed like a riverboat gambler: expensive oxblood boots, a frilled shirt of finespun linen, a fancy kid vest and an octagonal tie with a diamond pin. They were making their way across the wide street toward the livery.

"Well, now," Fargo said, "when it rains it pours. The angelic Miss Johanson."

Septimus slanted a curious glance toward him. "You know *her*, too? I figured you for a pussy hound, Buckskins, but, by Godfrey, that's mighty fast work for a fellow what sleeps in a stall."

"Who's the dandy with her?"

"Hardiman Burke? Ahh, he's alla time swaggering it around. Owns the Adams Express Company and the big gambling parlor on River Street. Hell, he don't know a mule from a burro, but he fancies hisself a big frontier nabob."

"Express company, huh?" Fargo said in a speculative tone.

"Ahuh. I don't cotton to that perfumed clothes pole. Makes his brag how he's gonna be gov'nor one a these days and rule the roost. 'Nuther one a them law-and-order sons a bitches. He's pushin' Mayor Reece for a law to make every man what rides into Saint Joe stack his guns."

"Every man except the greasy-sack pistoleros on his payroll, I'd wager."

Septimus stifled his answer as the couple entered the hard-packed yard and moved into earshot.

"G'day, Septimus," Burke greeted the liveryman briskly, his eyes sliding quickly over Fargo. "Is my calash ready?"

"Yep. All she needed was truing on the rear offside wheel. Told you it wouldn't require a blacksmith. Cost you eight bits."

"Excellent, excellent. It's such a fine day, Miss Johanson and I decided to drive out to Lookout Bluff."

Fargo, still seated on the wagon tongue, enjoyed a closer, longer inspection of the beauty. Her intensely blue eyes confronted him frankly, but with none of the wanton encouragement of Lily Reece. In this masculine and dreary livery yard, she stood out like a brass spittoon.

"Generally, sir," she said to him in a cool, detached manner, "men disguise their thoughts a bit more discreetly."

"I suppose most men do," Fargo replied. "I don't consider myself rude, miss, just a bit untutored in civility and certainly overwhelmed in my senses. Please forgive me, and do bear in mind that thoughts are not hanging offenses."

Whatever she expected, this reply was not it. Again she gave him that ambiguous twitch of her fine, expressive lips—either a smile that died aborning or the trace of a dismissive frown.

Hardiman Burke overheard all this but was too worldly to rear up on his hind legs as Jack Parsons had done. He eyed Fargo as he might a mangy dog lying in his path.

"I see you're loaded for bear, mister. You won't need all those weapons in Saint Joe. They'll only get you in trouble. Our sheriff doesn't think too highly of border ruffians, and he's a good man to let alone."

Fargo had met Burke's type often in boomtowns—a man far more important than meritorious. And quite possibly "our sheriff" was on Burke's payroll.

"Well, then, I promise to leave him alone," Fargo replied.

Burke narrowed his eyes, scrutinizing Fargo with more attention, then led Inge around to the rear of the livery where his calash was parked.

Septimus, busy watching Inge's swaying hips, loosed a fluming sigh. "She ain't just pure satin, Buckskins—she's got sprites in her eyes like no calico I ever seen. Calm as a summer pond on the outside, but she's got the flame within, that gal has."

"*I* didn't feel too much heat. Matter fact, I'd say she pisses icicles."

"Jever wonder what it'd be like to ride a gal like that till she's throwing off sparks?"

"Tell you what—I'll soon let you know."

Septimus looked at him askance. "You *mean* that, don'tcha?"

"I ain't the one who prefers knotholes, Dad."

"You crazy bastard! That gal is parlor-mannered—quotes books, got her a Chinese servant, and stays in the fanciest room in the Patee House. The only men who get close to *her* are rolling in it. She don't waste her time on saddle tramps. 'Sides all that . . ."

Septimus watched the calash round the corner of the livery and head into the street.

"'Sides all that," he resumed, "you ruffled ol' Hardiman's feathers good when you sassed Inge. I was you, I'd ease off them two. He's one to keep accounts."

"Good," Fargo replied. "That's just hunky-dory with me because I'm one to settle them."

Something in this quiet, confident reply made Septimus study the younger man again. "Say, quit taking me for a sleigh ride. How's come all the damn questions? You harped all over me for nosing into things. I . . ."

Again he trailed off. "Christ, how could I curry that fine stallion and not figure it out. You're the Trailsman, ain'tcher?"

"Skye Fargo, all the way down to the ground."

"Ahuh. Well, then, I believe what you said about settling accounts, Fargo. But *ground* is all you're likely to get around Saint Joe—'bout six feet of it."

5

Fargo spent most of that afternoon scouting the country around Saint Joseph in thorough, ever-widening circles, getting the lay of the land and making a mind map. His life may soon depend on a good knowledge of this terrain, and hard experience had taught him that unscouted country was the most dangerous.

He had also learned that scouting was much more than merely looking at the terrain. By long habit he avoided sending his eye out to seize one image. Instead, he let all the images "come up to his eyes." Only then could he pick out the ones that truly mattered.

This section of northwest Missouri could work for or against a man. At points the sandy bluffs overlooking the wide emerald green river provided excellent vantage points where he could see for miles. But the hilly, heavily wooded ground beyond the tableland was bristling with coverts and caves ideal for sheltering men of "no church conscience."

At one point Fargo rode up a steep bluff about three miles downriver of Saint Joseph and immediately spotted a ragtag army of Pukes—pro-slavery militiamen—camped on the Kansas side. The national debate between abolitionists and slavers had come to a head in Missouri and Kansas, where both sides used the issue to kill, rape and plunder. Fargo knew every state and territory in the American West, and none—not even the bloody part of Texas known as *Comancheria*—rivaled this region for mayhem, terror and violence.

Jude Lattimer's gang, and the powers behind them, mirrored that wide-open violence. Most express robbers, in Fargo's experience, wanted only the swag—murder was a last resort. Lattimer's bunch, however, routinely killed drivers, messenger guards and even military escorts. Superior numbers against the gang didn't matter because of unerring marksmanship and the brilliance of their planning.

And since Jude Lattimer and his fellow curly wolves hardly struck Fargo as men of high mentality, the brilliance came from elsewhere. Pinkerton's words from earlier echoed in Fargo's mind: *This unknown mastermind runs his criminal empire without direct involvement.*

When Fargo could fit only four fingers between the horizon and the sun, he reversed his dust back toward Saint Joe, avoiding the well-graded Overland stage road and instead following a narrow, grassy lane. He gave the Ovaro his head and let him open out from a lope to a gallop, then a blistering run, knowing the stallion would take the stall easier later. There were too many horse thieves hanging around jumping-off places, and Fargo dared not leave the Ovaro in a paddock overnight.

"Message runner come for you," Septimus greeted him when Fargo led his stallion, bit flecked with foam, into the big livery barn. "Says your uncle Pete wants to see you at eight sharp."

Fargo nodded. He loosed the cinch and pulled his saddle, pad and blanket, then dropped bit and bridle. He threw a halter and lead line on the stallion and led him out to the paddock, walking him in circles to cool him out.

Septimus followed them outside. "Ask me, you don't strike me as a jasper who even has an uncle. And iffen you did, he'd likely be pressing beaver pelts into packs and fightin' featherheads out in Zeb Pike country."

Fargo ignored the old salt's fishing trip. Allan Pinkerton was death on codes and cute messages, and this one was a summons to a meeting.

Septimus realized he'd overstepped. "Then again," he added, "when it comes to kin, I got none either. There's times when I think mebbe a bird shit on a rock and I hatched from the sun."

Fargo continued circling with the Ovaro, his eyes in constant scanning motion. "I don't worry about any man's family or roots, old roadster. Where we're going is more important than where we came from."

"Ahuh, that shines. Say, I will allow as how this stallion is prime horseflesh. But there ain't one helluva difference twixt him and them bangtails I use to break to leather down in New Mex. And *them* sons a bitches was man-killers till I choked and water-starved 'em. You don't even wear spurs—how do you control this animal?"

"Generally I don't. You might say our dispositions match up good."

Septimus chuckled. "I hope that don't mean *you're* gonna bite me on the hinder, too. Thissen's got me twice now."

The old codger hooked a thumb toward the barrel where he kept his jug. "Anti-fogmatic? Help yourself."

This time Fargo handed the line to Septimus and pulled the jug out, knocking back a slug of the potent brew. Instantly his eyes filmed. "Christ, Septimus—this panther piss makes Taos Lightning taste like lemonade."

The hostler snorted. "For a man big enough to fight cougars with a shoe, you ain't no great shakes at imbibin' liquor."

Fargo handed him the jug and took the line back from him. "Liquor? Old son, that witch's brew is laced with strychnine."

"Aye, it's Indian burner," Septimus admitted. "Make a man outta you. Say . . . Inge and Hardiman come back 'bout an hour afore you. I wunner what they done out to Lookout Bluff?"

"If you're hinting at slap and tickle," Fargo said, "she doesn't strike me as the type to point her heels to the sky in a conveyance—especially in broad daylight."

"Naw, that shines. *She* ain't no painted cat—she beats the rest of 'em all hollow. They say her rooms at the Patee even got a whatchacallit, an indoor convenience."

"Besides that message boy," Fargo said casually, changing the subject, "anybody else come 'round today asking for me?"

"Nope. You expecting trouble?"

"Who said a damn thing about trouble?"

The old man laughed so hard he coughed up phlegm. "Shit, boy, don't play the soft-brain with me. Trouble is the street you live on."

"You've got a *few* teeth left," Fargo reminded him. "That could change."

"Ahh, no need to go on the scrap. Nobody come askin' for you. But they was a big, mean-around-the-mouth bastard watching this place from the street."

"Did he have little pig eyes and a teamster's mustache?"

"Naw. He was a hatchet head with one a the ugliest scars I ever seen—ran clear from his ear to his jaw."

Jude Lattimer, Fargo thought. But was he here to parley or smoke me down?

"You're mixing with some rough-lookin' hard cases," Septimus added. "I hope you know what the hell you're doing."

"Don't get ahead of the facts," Fargo said, letting it go.

Each man was alone with his thoughts for a minute or two. Then Septimus abruptly cursed.

"It makes me wrathy, Fargo. That scarred-up hombre out in the street, larceny in his eyes—back east is called the land of steady habits. Out west it's the land of get-rich-quick fever. Sure, most of these hay-footed pilgrims outfittin' here in Saint Joe are God-fearin' folks who just want a better life for their youngens. But there's more and more grifters and killers and easy-money lemmings showin' up each day, and *them* sons a bitches will queer the whole deal for the rest."

Fargo expelled a long sigh, nodding. "Just maybe it's the way you say, old campaigner. The two-bit killers and road agents and such can be reined in— there's more good men than bad. But I got a God-fear of these 'barons' and speculators— I ain't so certain they can be stopped. A fish rots from the top."

By now Septimus had quickly dried off the Ovaro and started in on his tangled mane with a metal-toothed curry-comb. Fargo set off on foot through a freight alley, angling toward the center of town.

Keeping his eye to all sides, and throwing glances over his shoulder, Fargo searched out a barbershop that sold baths for four bits. After he'd scrubbed up he had his hair and beard trimmed and went the whole hog, tossing in an extra dime for the lilac water.

By now his stomach was rumbling. He aimed toward the commerce section near the river and found the Hog's Breath saloon doing a lively trade.

"Scrape the gravy skillet, Katy!" he greeted the proprietress, squeezing in at the long front counter and placing his elbows carefully to avoid the beer slops. "Got any steaks?"

"Huh! The pilgrims have bought up all the butcher beef. All I got left is ham-and-bean soup with dumplings and hot biscuits."

Fargo planked a gold dollar. "Sounds jake to me. Draw me a beer, too, and—"

"And make it nappy," she finished for him, laughing. "I've seen how you pout when there ain't a good head on it."

Fargo had felt watched ever since riding back to town. While he tied into his meal, he relied on the back-bar mirror to study every man who entered. He was grateful that Saint Joe was a bustling staging-out area, not an isolated crossroads settlement where strangers drew sharp notice. Even his buckskins—fringes black with old blood—excited little notice. And so many men packed weapons that his brass-framed Henry rifle hardly drew a glance in this busy transportation center.

While Fargo was sopping up the last of his soup with a biscuit, a vendor wearing a sack suit and a straw boater made the rounds trying to sell Indian-skull doorstops to the greenhorns.

"Safe on the reservation at last!" he greeted Fargo, holding a brightly painted skull out for his inspection. "Only two dollars. Wonderful conversation piece, friend. Every one of 'em killed fair and square on the battlefield."

"Most likely," Fargo replied, "that was a cracker-and-molasses Indian who died of yellow fever on a reservation. There's plenty for the taking."

Katy spotted the drummer and shook a fist at him. "Henry, you damn ghoul, I told you before—get them brainpans out of my place!"

Henry hoisted his burlap bag of grisly wares onto a shoulder and stalked out, muttering something about Injun lovers.

Katy moved down and leaned across the counter, speaking just above a whisper. "C'mon, Skye. Tell Curious Kate why a fellow who prefers to ride the high lonesome back of beyond has come to *this* Sodom? It can't be my cooking."

"Don't wager on that," Fargo gainsaid. "That biscuit I just finished was so light I had to hold it down."

"Uh-hunh, cut the soft soap. Last time you were here you raised one hell of a ruckus, and I 'magine you will again."

Fargo assumed a cherub's face. "You know how it is with me—live and let live."

"Sure, until it's kill or be killed."

"There's that," Fargo agreed, and they both laughed.

Katy's plump cheeks turned down at the corners of her mouth when she suddenly frowned. "No joshing now, you have a mighty nice face. I hope it won't end up on a reward dodger—or worse yet, painted red with undertaker's rouge."

By the time Fargo left the Hog's Breath, the bloodred sun was sinking lower beyond the river, the shadows purpling and flattening out. His premonitory "truth goose" was back— a slight tingle on the back of his neck warning him of imminent danger.

He regretted not using the Indian tunnel again. The high false-fronts blocked the last feeble rays of the sun and threw the street into blue-black shadow, illuminated only weakly by sporadic coal-oil streetlamps. It was thus easy for unidentified men to flow easily in the obscure, shape-shifting shadows.

Fargo passed a Chinese laundry, a harness shop and a huge outfitter's emporium doing a brisk business as soon-to-depart pilgrims stocked up on pots, pans, clothing, axes and other items for the long trek to Oregon and California. Saint Joe had few boardwalks yet, which meant Fargo could not listen for the loud thump of bootheels following him. He was forced to constantly cast backward glances.

But trying to isolate figures in the lowering gloom was like trying to separate the water from the wet. When Fargo heard the flat metallic click of a hammer being cocked behind him, the sound scraped along his spine like a rusty rake. Cool sweat broke out on his temples and he abruptly ducked into an alley.

Moving swiftly, he hid behind a dray wagon and shifted his Henry to his left hand, shucking out his Colt with the right. In the near total darkness it was impossible to make out the figure standing in the mouth of the alley. But the Trailsman heard the steady rise and fall of his breathing.

It was Fargo's way to cure a boil by lancing it. But the street behind the mystery stalker was too crowded and Fargo wanted to avoid a cartridge session.

"Howdy, Jacky boy," he called out from only a few feet away. "Looking for me?"

Fargo braced for a spray of lead. Instead, the startled figure instantly faded like a wraith into the dark maw of the night.

Fargo waited a full minute, then leathered his shooter.

"Interesting," he muttered. Then he set out for the meeting with Pinkerton.

6

Fargo arrived a few minutes early for the meeting and found Pinkerton writing at his giant mahogany desk.

"My daily client reports," he explained, nodding Fargo toward a chair in front of the desk. "I've discovered that a client will bear almost any expense if he gets a daily summary of his case and accounting of his funds. That's why I only hire operatives who can write well—it's more important than skilled marksmanship."

"Do tell? Well, if you expect me to—"

Pinkerton waved him silent. "You are an exception in a desperate situation, Fargo. Even Shakespeare's writing talent couldn't crack this nut open. By the way—*can* you read and write?"

"After a fashion. You saw me sign our contract. So who's the client in this case?"

"Technically, my primary client is the U.S. government, but that's our secret. Locally, it's Hardiman Burke, owner of the Adams Express and Freighting Company. It's named for his former partner Clinton Adams, who . . . shall we say, died under rather unusual circumstances about six months ago. Adams Express has been robbed twice now for modest losses, and— What in the devil are you grinning about?"

Fargo slid a skinny black Mexican cigar from his pocket, stuck it between his teeth, and lifted the chimney of the lamp on Pinkerton's desk. He got the cigar glowing good before he replied.

"I met Burke today at the livery, is all. He's a jackass. Hinted around that I carry too many weapons for my own good."

"Well, stay out of his way," Pinkerton snapped in his trilling brogue, frowning. "He is indeed a jackass. But I also consider him a suspect in this express-robber operation."

Fargo gave his employer a puzzleheaded look. "He hired you, didn't he?"

"What's that to the matter? I've pored over the newspaper and law-enforcement accounts of Clinton Adams's death, and I don't credit the claim that he died in an accidental fire."

"You figure Burke had him murdered because Adams was too honest?"

"There's no evidence of that, but it happens with alarming frequency this far west. These gold shipments are no personal loss to him. Both robberies were of U.S. Treasury consignments, so it's the American people who pay the freight, literally."

"Yeah, I take your drift. And if he didn't put up a front by hiring you it'd look a mite queer, I reckon."

"He's *only* a suspect," Pinkerton qualified. "One of several. And I only include him because of clear signs of inside cooperation. In any event, you just keep your nose out of that part of the pie. I have two experienced operatives working the angles in and around Saint Joseph."

"Yeah, they can both write and use silverware," Fargo barbed. "I'm just the ignorant meat that feeds the tiger."

"Bosh! Your end of it is both dangerous and important. Speaking of your end—has Lattimer made further contact with you?"

"That's a poser. According to the old codger who runs the livery, a jasper fitting Lattimer's description was hanging around near the livery while I was gone. But he didn't ask for me."

Pinkerton frowned as he blotted his report with sand. "Well, we can't force his hand. It's only been a day since you surprised him in his camp. But dash it all, I *need* a man inside that ring. The situation here in town seems to have reached an impasse."

Somebody rapped out the "shave-and-a-haircut" signal on the alley door. A second later it was opened and a string-bean-thin man with an utterly unremarkable moon face stepped inside.

"Skye Fargo," Pinkerton said, "meet John Fowler, formerly constable of Saint Louis. But from here on out you'll know him publicly as Jess Singer, a drummer for the Stanton Company out of Cleveland, purveyors of ladies' notions."

"It's a pleasure, Fargo," the former lawman said, extending a limp and clammy hand.

"Skye," Pinkerton said, "you are an exception to my general rule. I try to hire brave men who don't *look* particularly brave. John Fowler is one of the bravest, but one look at his weak chin and watery eyes, and the hard cases dismiss him as mild and harmless. I assure you that his intelligence, courage and physical prowess belie his mild and diffident manner."

Fargo's lips twitched into a grin. "Allan, you're preaching to the converted. I once watched this 'weak sister' cut down Ace Ludlow and his brain-sick brother, Dave, in front of the Gold Room in Saint Louis. Fair fight, too, with all the bullet holes in front. This rake handle is tough as a two-bit steak. But he was heeled in those days."

"Oh, I still am," Fowler said, opening his corduroy coat. He wore a black-handled Remington in a chamois holster under his left armpit. "Same barking iron I killed the Ludlow brothers with. Allan doesn't permit open carrying, and now I've got so I don't like to flash the artillery."

"Each man to his own gait. I like to give a man fair warning. But I can see how a hideout gun might be more useful in your line of work."

"It's *your* line of work now, too," Pinkerton reminded him.

Fargo grinned, squinting as smoke curled into his eyes. "That's right—I'm a genuine Pinkerton man. A by-God operative with a tin whistle and a dark lantern. I'm just curious, chief—which one of my eyes is allowed to sleep?"

Pinkerton gave him a pitying look. "Just remember what you promised me earlier today—that you'll play it by *my* rules."

"Insofar as possible," Fargo qualified.

Fowler laughed. "No point in getting your bristles up, Allan. When you hired Skye Fargo, you leased a little piece of hell. Expect the heat to rise."

"By the way," Fargo said, "where's this female operative you mentioned? Don't I get to meet her? I smell better now."

"All in good time," Pinkerton said evasively. "She's on duty now."

"Wait until you glom this little sugarplum," Fowler put in. "I don't stand a snowball's chance, but you, Fargo, just might get a little frippet if you—"

"Ahem! Don't encourage him," Pinkerton cut in sternly. "Coals to Newcastle and all that. He'd just be wasting his time anyway. Besides, Fargo, I have another female in mind for you, and a real looker—albeit a dangerous one. Knowing her could prove useful—she seems to have a bizarre liaison with none other than Jack Parsons. And her father is another suspect."

Fargo had been balanced on the hind legs of his chair. Now the front legs came crashing down. "You don't mean Lily Reece, the mayor's hellcat daughter?"

Fowler grinned; Pinkerton looked astonished. "Only one day in town and you've met *her*, too? Is that cod of yours a bloodhound?"

"It was a chance meeting," Fargo said, leaving out the fight with Parsons—Pinkerton wouldn't approve. "Besides, she's hard to miss."

"Well, if she wasn't so rich she'd be considered an adventuress. But I'm not certain if she's just a wild woman in fancy feathers or something worse."

"We know she's making the two-backed beast with Jack Parsons," Fowler chimed in. "And *that* son of a bitch could walk under a snake's belly on stilts."

"Yeah, that's got me treed," Fargo admitted. "'Strumpet' or 'spitfire' don't quite cover a woman that reckless. But I got a hunch she's not in cahoots with Parsons and the gang."

"I'm not intimating that she is," Pinkerton said. "It's her father I'm worried about. My investigations show that he's been buying up huge parcels of land back east, and it's not clear where he's getting the money. Certainly not from his six-hundred-dollar-a-year salary as mayor. So she *could* have met Parsons through him."

"I didn't think of that," Fargo admitted.

"It's just a theory. Politicians have their hands in many pots. At any rate, don't engage the mayor in any way—John runs his traps regularly and he has reasonably good informants. But see what you can find out from the girl. Even if she's in the dark, she may inadvertently spill something."

"But gird your loins, Romeo," Fowler warned. "I hear Lily Reece likes to put her men through their facings. There's rumors she likes to have the whip hand—literally."

"Bosh," Pinkerton scoffed. "Foolish pub lore."

"So Hardiman Burke and Mayor Josiah Reece are on your list," Fargo prodded. "Anybody else?"

Pinkerton seemed to retreat within himself for a long moment, his face troubled. Then: "Yes, but I'm not yet ready to name him. I'm more disposed to respect him and give him the benefit of the doubt."

"All right," Fargo said, "but do either of you gents have any way in hell of knowing when the next heist might happen—or where?"

"No, damn it to hell!" Pinkerton swore. "It could be Adams Express next time or one of three other express lines linking the Comstock mines to Washington City. Missouri is a hub for all four of them."

"That's where you figure into the mix, Fargo," Fowler said. "If you can bamboozle Lattimer and get into his gang, he'll have to tell you sooner or later."

"And since Jack Parsons is one of Lily Reece's favorites," Pinkerton reminded the Trailsman, "she might be useful—especially if her father is the secret mastermind."

Fargo nodded. "I see how the wind sets. Lily Reece doesn't strike me as the type to lip salt out of a man's hand, but she's already invited me to come visit her—and I don't get the impression she's got a taffy pull in mind."

Fowler snorted. Pinkerton sent him a quelling stare. "It's no matter for levity, John. So far the butcher's bill has been steep, gentlemen. We *must* put the kibosh on this ring as quickly as possible."

"As for Lattimer," Fargo said, picking up an earlier thread, "I can't figure the angles with that crafty son of a buck. He says I'm in, but he could just be stringing me along until he gets the chance to douse my glims."

"Well, if that's so," Fowler put in, "and *if* Hardiman Burke is in cahoots with Lattimer's bunch, don't turn your back on him, either. Burke may look like a sachet kitten, but there's hard bark under his perfume. Knows how to use a lead-chucker, too."

"I second that warning," Pinkerton said. "Fargo, this is dangerous for all of us, but you've got the little end of the horn. You've got a reputation for staying alive in hard situations, but you'll need all of your skills for this job—and also a good ration of luck."

Fargo ground his cigar butt out on a bootheel, not liking the turn this trail was taking. First Katy at the Hog's Breath, then Septimus, now John Fowler and Pinkerton—four people issuing grave warnings to him in one day. Fargo wasn't superstitious, but this didn't bode well.

He couldn't help recalling the recently defunct Pony Express, which originated here in Saint Joe and became famous for its help-wanted notice:

WANTED:
Young, skinny, wiry fellows.
Must be expert riders.
Willing to risk death daily.
ORPHANS PREFERRED

Fargo and John Fowler slipped out of Pinkerton's office a few minutes apart, Fargo crossing the Hannibal and Saint Joseph Railroad tracks and bearing toward Enterprise Street in the heart of town.

Again he had the tingling sense that he was being followed, but was it really a jealous Parsons or was it Jude Lattimer himself, looking to kill an intruder who knew too much?

Number seventeen Enterprise Street occupied a huge lot in a block of fine houses built by the first capital-rich settlers of Saint Joseph. Fargo took in a two-story brick edifice with lancet-arched windows and a wraparound veranda in the Southern style. Chinaberry trees and neatly manicured shrubbery lined a flagstone path leading to the wide front steps.

Fargo was only a few feet away from the steps when cold steel kissed the back of his neck.

"That's a bowie," Fargo said, his voice calmer than his

fear-hammering heart. "Twelve-inch blade, am I right, Dog Man?"

Willy "Dog Man" Lee chuckled behind him. "Right as the mail, Fargo. I could whack your head off right now, pickle it in brine, and sell it for a thousand simoleons."

Fargo silently cursed himself for stupidly walking into this trap.

"Looks like Lattimer wants me in the gang," he said. "Otherwise you'd've killed me by now."

The sharp pressure on his neck eased and Fargo turned slowly around to confront the half-breed in the oily yellow light spilling from the house. Dog Man's cauliflower ear looked like a lump of misshapen sealing wax. His sawed-off 12-gauge now depended from his left shoulder in a canvas rig.

"Hell, I got no desire to kill you, Fargo. It's Jack wants to put you under, and sure as cats fighting he'll try. He's madder 'n a peeled rattler. You cracked his only good jaw tooth when you give him that sockdologer earlier. Now he means to flay your soles. Specially since you gelded him in front of his redheaded whore."

"Then I'm surprised it's you out here instead of him."

"Don't be so sure he ain't out here. You here to diddle his she-bitch?"

"If the line ain't too long," Fargo said, and Dog Man laughed as he slid the bowie into its beadwork sheath.

"I ain't in line," Dog Man assured him. "She don't put out for 'breeds. Swears we got red jizzum. Ain't no way in hell I'd bull her even if she let me. You best get set for a ripsnorter, Fargo. When that crazy bitch gets done with you, you'll need a doctor—or a pine box."

"Rough, huh?"

Dog Man whistled. "Rough? Trooper, I spied through the window once while her and Parsons done the black act. She worked him like a peeler taming a man-killer. Christ, I couldn't get a boner for a week, she scairt me so much."

"You got me curious now."

"Your funeral. Anyhow, Jude says you're in the gang. But he'll keep an eye on you just to make sure. For now just lay low and stay at the livery. I'll be coming to fetch you soon. Here."

He handed Fargo another double eagle. "I'll lay my cards out right now, Fargo. Jude thinks you're on the square—that story about topping his sister was pure genius. But I know better. You plan to either send us to prison or kill us."

"Doesn't that make you a fool for not killing me on the spot?"

Dog Man's mouth curled into a lopsided grin. "Eventually I'll get around to that. But you're an entertaining jasper, and life gets mighty boresome on the owlhoot trail. I plan to enjoy watching you do the hurt dance on us."

A moment later Dog Man had melted into the shadows.

7

"Well, now," Lily Reece said when she answered Fargo's knock. "I was wondering why you were taking so long to come see me. Most men would have followed me home like hungry dogs after that invite I gave you. I do hope you're not . . . timid?"

Fargo followed her inside, noticing how her thin linen wrapper—obviously all she wore—revealed her sweeping curves and the outline of her impressive, high-split ass.

"Timid?" Fargo repeated. "Lady, when you met me earlier I smelled like a bear's cave. I figured you'd appreciate me having a bath since you suggested it."

She stopped in the entrance hall to sniff him. "Phew! Toilet water? Candidly, I preferred your smell earlier. I didn't take you for the lilac-water type."

"If you'd like, I can go have a quick roll in horse shit."

"No. Now I've got you here, I'm getting my use of you. Besides, an *amour fou* should be spontaneous and wild."

She led her visitor into a sumptuous parlor with a rose-pattern carpet, leather wing chairs, a big fieldstone fireplace with a green marble mantel, and fancy crystal lamps in brass wall sconces. She steered him toward a big chintz-covered sofa bristling with French-stitched satin pillows. One hell of a layout, Fargo figured, for a man supposedly making six hundred a year.

A carafe filled with topaz-colored bourbon sat on a gilt-edged table in front of the sofa. She poured them each a glass while Fargo propped his Henry against one end of the sofa.

"Here's to a tomcat on the prowl," she toasted him, "and his queen in heat."

Fargo tossed the liquor back, then grinned broadly as he

dropped his hat on the table. "Now see, that's what I like. A woman who skips the dickering and states her best offer right off."

She stood up, shimmying out of the thin wrapper and letting it fall in a puddle at her feet. "You like what's being offered?"

Fargo's appreciative gaze raked over her from the fiery hair and emerald eyes, past a pair of puffy loaves with big plum nipples, to a tapering "V" of sienna mons hair that pointed his eyes even farther south to the very beginning of her slit.

"Most redheads have a scratchy bush," she said, her voice going husky as lust and excitement gripped her. "But feel mine."

Fargo did. "Pure French wool," he assured her.

"Like what you see?" she demanded again.

Fargo felt J. Henry stirring to life like a snake uncoiling. "Would a cow lick Lot's wife?"

"Well, then, may I lick *you*?"

"With me," Fargo replied, unbuckling his gun belt, "it's always the lady's choice. Lick it, suck it, kiss it, take a few careful nibbles if you like."

"No," she said, suddenly producing a quirt from under one of the cushions and snapping it. "I mean may I *lick* you?"

Fargo, who had dallied with all manner of women with strange requests, was nonetheless astonished. So all the tall talk about Lily was true? Fargo had serviced two women at once, had twisted into every position possible for human anatomy and—on one memorable occasion—even screwed a woman on the galloping Ovaro's back until they were both bucked off. But this was a bizarre new turn in the erotic trail.

He looked at her askance, noticing how ragged her breathing had grown as she anticipated the fulfillment of her "*amour fou.*"

"Say now—nice kitty, rough tongue. You measure corn by your own bushel, I see."

Her voice suddenly sounded frustrated. "Oh, I get it. It's always the lady's choice with you until the lady's choice is too sick for your conventional tastes?"

"It's a mite queer," Fargo said. "But I wouldn't 'xactly call it sick."

"My lands! So maybe you *will* expand your horizons?"

"Speaking of expanding . . ." Fargo opened his fly and freed his throbbing, bobbing manhood. It leaped up and down with his heartbeats, the tip a swollen bluish-purple knob.

Lily's eyes widened. "Jerusalem! That's quite a war club, Fargo! I've never seen size like that on a creature with only two legs."

"You won't be requiring that quirt to get het up," Fargo assured her, taking it from her hand and tossing it aside. He knocked a few pillows out of the way. "Just lay down and spread those legs wide. Your trouble is, you ain't met a man who knows how to make you come good. I'm gonna do you hard and deep, girl, make you forget all about lashing my ass."

The sexual power balance had abruptly shifted from Lily to this well-hung stallion now mesmerizing her.

"Oh, yes," she said breathlessly, dropping onto her back. "I don't like these gallant gentlemen, Fargo, who keep time to the church bells. I want a bull in the hot moons—that's why I let clumsy brutes like Jack Parsons root on me. But he pops off in about one minute, and I never get my shiver even when I skin his ass good first."

"Now we can't have that," Fargo promised her. He took her left leg and hooked it over the back of the sofa. This opened up an exciting view of the glistening petals and folds of her sex, the mysterious hole at her center open wide like a hungry, begging mouth.

He climbed into his favorite saddle, lined up his shaft perfectly with her belly mouth, and flexed his ass hard, coaxing a surprised cry of pleasure out of her as he parted and penetrated the velvet tightness.

"Oh, Fargo, you stallion! It feels like you're up in my chest! Oh, Jesus, *what* are you doing . . . ?"

Speech failed her, sheer, mindless delirium taking over, as Fargo rocked hard and fast into the deepest wet of her, surprising her with a male prowess she'd never dreamed existed. For Fargo, it had been too damn long since he'd enjoyed the mazy waltz—and he knew this eccentric, unfulfilled woman needed it even harder and faster than most horny vixens, so that's how he gave it to her.

Her cries climbed the scale of octaves as Fargo rogered her roundly, the force of his thrusts inching the big sofa into motion. Lily, panting like an overheated animal, suddenly bent like an archer's bow as a string of body-twitching climaxes racked her. Fargo finished strong, spending himself deep inside her and then collapsing atop her, chest heaving.

The intensity of their release left both of them adrift in a timeless, wordless daze for uncounted minutes. Finally Lily's voice pulled Fargo back to the present.

"My lands, I feel I owe you a stud fee. How about pouring us another drink?"

The moment Fargo rolled onto one hip, reaching for the carafe, a sharp *whap* split the silence, and fire licked his ass.

"You devious little bitch!" He caught her wrist before she could quirt him again.

"My goodness, Dr. Fargo! You can't expect just one treatment to cure me completely."

Fargo grinned. "Yeah, I see this is a challenging case. Let's slip you another dose."

He rolled back into the saddle and made her take her medicine again. This time the acrobatic treatment left both of them a confused tangle of limbs, dazed and mindless even longer.

Fargo finally sat up and tucked his sated manhood back behind his fly. She didn't expect his next remark. "I hear your old man is the mayor?"

"Did you look that up in the almanac?" she said in a sleepy voice. "Daddy dearest is many things, Fargo."

"Yeah? So what else is he?"

Fargo regretted the question when her big green eyes grew suddenly shrewd. "What's that to you, long-tall?"

"Well, I've never seen a mayor's daughter naked, is all. This is an occasion for me."

"Mmm . . . well, you're a well-practiced liar, but I suspect you've seen more naked women than a midwife. What are you up to?"

"You're the one who said your father is many things. I'm just a mite curious what you meant."

She sat up, smiled at Fargo, then plucked her wrapper off the floor and stood up to slip it back on. Again Fargo admired her polished-ivory ass and the tantalizing dimples at the base of her spine.

"For one thing," she said, "he's a self-made man, and every day he thanks his Creator. For another, he's a horny old goat. He put my mother into an early grave with all his chasing after women my age. Right now he's making a fool of himself over a high-toned blonde who wouldn't deign to wipe her ass with him if he wasn't lousy with money. And I mean *lousy* money. She's got him and a couple other horny, middle-aged fools hot to bed her."

"A high-toned blonde," Fargo repeated. "Sounds like the lovely Miss Inge strikes again."

Lily's ripe-fruit lips parted in amusement. "Oh, so you've already sniffed her out? Well, I'm sure she'd enjoy strapping a buck like you on after all those suet guts she runs with. But you won't tap *her* little hidey-hole unless you come into a considerable fortune."

Her sarcastic remark about Josiah Reece's "lousy" money had piqued Fargo's curiosity. But this fiery redhead was as smart as she was horny, and Fargo had pushed things too far already.

"A gold digger, I can understand," Fargo said. "And I don't fault a woman for negotiating with what she's got. It does beat all, though, that a looker like you would prefer an ugly farmer's bull like Jack Parsons."

"I told you, I will not abide a milquetoast male. I'm not the girl for courting and sparking. No flowers, no candy, just a hard rawhiding."

Parsons . . . now that Fargo had a little blood back in his brain, he thought of that encounter earlier in the alley.

"Lady's choice," Fargo surrendered. "But some things you step in are hard to wipe off. That dumb bastard is jealous of you, and he's the type who won't just fade when you're ready for the next bull."

For the first time since Fargo's arrival her confidence

seemed to ebb. "Yes, I've begun to realize that. I think he's one of those pathetic wretches who'll tell me, 'If I can't have you, no man will.' I just might have to kill him."

Fargo, jolted by her casual remark, opened his mouth to reply. Just then, however, he noticed something ominous: The steady singsong of insect noise outside the house had suddenly fallen silent.

"Shit," he muttered, "here's the fandango."

He grabbed Lily and threw her to the floor only moments before one of the tall parlor windows exploded inward in shards. Three shots in rapid succession ripped into the sofa, one of the pillows coughing feathers. Fargo, covering Lily with his body, stabbed for his Colt and fired back through the shattered window. A moment later he heard running footsteps fade into the darkness.

Lily's cool, cynical detachment seemed shaken. She lay flat as Fargo moved quickly around the parlor, turning down all but one of the wall lamps.

"The mayor won't like *this*," she said, a quaver in her voice as Fargo helped her up. "That window glass was shipped in from Kansas City. And now there's bullet holes in the sofa he had freighted from Boston."

"Let him think it was drunks hoo-rawing the town," Fargo suggested. "What time does he generally come home?"

"He'll be gambling and speechifying for another three hours, at least."

"You got a gun?"

She nodded.

"I don't think Parsons will be back tonight. But I'd keep that gun cocked and in my hand."

Fargo snatched up his Henry. Lily sent him an odd look in the dim, flickering light. "Are you sure it was Parsons?"

"Aren't you?"

"It's likely. But you're trouble, Skye Fargo. Anybody can see that just by looking into that tough, handsome face of yours and those trouble-seeking blue eyes. You didn't come to Saint Joseph just to squire the ladies—you're up to something dangerous, and for all I know that attack just now might have had nothing to do with me or a jealous brute. It could be anybody who wants you dead."

8

Fargo bedded down in an empty stall at the livery, sleeping on his Henry. But the only disturbance was Septimus Perkins, who passed out drunk around midnight and snored until dawn with a racket like a boar in rut.

Fargo arrived at the Hog's Breath early, knowing that Katy's delicious cooking sold out early. He feasted on ham, eggs and grits swimming in butter, washing it all down with cold applejack. Before he had even saucered and blown his coffee, John Fowler ambled in, straw sample case in hand.

Fargo had told Pinkerton and Fowler where he could usually be found during breakfast and agreed to treat them as strangers in public. Fowler purchased several boiled eggs and dropped them into his pocket. As he turned to leave, the skinny, nondescript man in a stiff black bowler hat—known as Jess Singer around town—stuck a cheap clay pipe between his teeth. He stopped for a moment where Fargo stood at the long front counter.

"Trouble you for a match, mister?"

Fargo dug into the possibles bag dangling from his belt and handed Fowler a lucifer match. As the detective reached for it he dropped a small piece of folded paper beside Fargo's empty plate.

Fargo palmed it and waited a few minutes after Fowler had left. He didn't read the message until he was back out on the street:

Ozark Hotel, Room 330. Use service entrance rear alley.

Fargo took a careful look around in the bright, cool, early sunshine making crisp shadows. He picked his way carefully across the wide street. Freight wagons with their six-foot wheels and one-inch-thick iron tires had left permanent ruts now filled with brackish water.

Mindful of last night's attack, he hugged the buildings close as he bore toward the river. He passed a general store with barrels of pickles and crackers out front, old men who had retired to the liar's bench sitting out front whittling. Next came a string of plush gambling houses whose gilt-letter signs advertised faro, poker, keno, monte and craps.

Closer to the east bank of the Missouri, the fancier gambling houses were replaced by shoddy clapboard saloons with sawbuck tables and puncheon floors covered in sawdust to absorb the tobacco spit. These establishments featured bare-knuckle boxing and dogfights. Although billed as entertainment, the real attraction was wagering on the outcome.

One saloon was a giant circus tent with at least twenty horses tied to the long snortin' post out front. Clearly a magnet for debauchery on a large scale, it had attracted a few sourfaced Temperance biddies. They marched in a circle out front carrying signs that proclaimed DEMON DRINK and GOD'S LAST NAME ISN'T DAMN IT!

The Ozark, which squatted on River Street, was a drab three-story building sandwiched between a brick warehouse and a rickety steamboat landing. Casting one last, long glance around, Fargo slipped around to the rear entrance.

He found himself in a narrow ground-floor hallway that reeked of onions and whiskey. Fargo spotted stairs at the opposite end and made it up to Fowler's door without encountering anyone.

Fowler answered the trio of knocks immediately. "Morning, Trailsman. Enter my humble abode."

It was humble, all right, Fargo decided after a cursory glance around. The room was cramped, dingy and mildewed, with one flyspecked sash window and a bare plank floor. The legs of a narrow iron bedstead had been set in bowls of kerosene to keep off the bedbugs.

"You take the chair. I'll sit on the bed," Fowler said.

"Christ, I'm better off spreading my blankets at the livery," Fargo remarked as he plopped down on a spindly ladder-back chair that creaked under his weight.

"Oh, there's no fancy built-in bathtub like at the Patee," Fowler replied. "The whale-oil lamp stinks and the mattress is barley straw. But you might consider this hotel if you stay in town. I got this room at a good lay—five dollars a week, light breakfast included."

"Hell, doesn't Pinkerton post the rent?"

"Surely you jest? He's a Scotsman. Tighter than a popcorn fart."

"So what's on the spit?" Fargo pressed him.

"For one thing I'm just curious. I was running my traps last night before I turned in, and I heard about the shooting affray at the Reece home. I figured you'd be at the center of it."

"The way you say." Fargo removed his hat and balanced it on his knee. "Far as shoot-outs, it was pee doodles. Looks like Jack Parsons got a burr under his saddle because I was visiting Lily."

"I figured as much. But it might not be too smart to let him force your hand into killing him."

Fargo nodded. "Yeah. I'd like to shoot that son of a bitch so full of holes the flies could get in and *buzz* him to death. But that would put the kibosh on my membership in the gang. I'll have to play that one with a wild card."

"So you believe you *are* in the gang?"

"Oh, I'm definitely a road agent now. If Lattimer wanted me dead, Dog Man had a perfect opportunity last night when he put me under the blade in front of Reece's house."

"Unless," Fowler pointed out, "Lattimer doesn't want you dead quite yet because he suspects you—in which case he might want to find out everything you know before he frees your soul. Dog Man's old man was a Cheyenne and he taught his kid the torture arts."

"Jesus," Fargo said, "you do know how to bring a room down. I didn't think of that, but you could be right."

Something else occurred to Fargo. "I'm a mite curious—how did Pinkerton find out Lattimer is the muscle of this operation?"

"We didn't know for sure it was Lattimer until you confirmed it for us two nights ago. Making him a prime suspect was just good detective work on Pinkerton's part. Actually,

Jack Parsons was the key. Allan keeps prodigious crime records, and he made a short list of the best cracksmen operating in the states and territories."

"Yeah, I saw all those dodgers he keeps in his office. Most lawmen use them for kindling. He studies them like holy writ."

Fowler nodded. "We picked ten and I memorized the faces. Eventually I spotted Parsons running around town with Lily Reece. Then you were sent for and did an amazing job of tracking them from the scene of the last heist. Over a week had passed, the trail grown cold as last night's mashed potatoes, yet you still found them."

"Without a magnifying glass," Fargo tossed in, and both men shared a laugh.

"Yeah, old Pinkie gets carried away with those damn foolish detective kits," Fowler admitted. "But he's no fool, not by a jugful. You'll catch a weasel asleep before you bamboozle *that* cute old boy."

"Bully for him, but *I'm* the one supposedly joining Lattimer's pack of wolves. I at least need to know when they plan to pull their next heist."

"I believe Pinkerton when he claims even he can't answer that yet. We do know that the U.S. Treasury is sending in gold bullion—exactly how much is anybody's guess—through the Missouri sector soon, and they dare not put it under military escort."

"That makes sense," Fargo allowed. "Some of these Jayhawker and Puke gangs are a hundred men strong and have more combat experience than these federal titty babies with their pants tucked into their boots. If they spot a federal escort, they'll know they've struck a bonanza."

"Exactly. So secrecy is the only option. That puts the Pinkerton Agency in a rum place. Now that Allan knows for sure who the road agents are, he can't just let them strike again—they're as ruthless as scalpers, and he can't have that on his conscience. Then again, if we move in too soon we may never crush the head of the snake."

"Speaking of that—you must have your own ideas about this syndicate," Fargo prompted. "Who do you think is the brains behind it?"

"Well, Hardiman Burke would seem most likely since he owns an express company that's been hit twice. If so, he might be in it with Reece. A mayor can be mighty handy for controlling local lawmen and finding out what they know and suspect. Trouble is, there's no damn evidence to collar anyone above Lattimer and his bunch."

Fargo mulled all this for a minute, eyebrows knitting in a frown. "I still have trouble believing Burke would hire the Pinkerton Agency if he's the head hound. Pinkerton can't be bought off like a U.S. marshal and he generally gets his man."

"Yeah, but it's also a smart move if he's confident he can thwart Pinkerton."

Fargo nodded. "Anyhow, what about this third suspect Pinkerton's got in mind?"

"I'm damned if I can pry that name loose from him yet. Allan's a queer fish sometimes."

Fargo narrowed his eyes. "Yeah, well, speaking of prying names loose—"

Fowler grinned and raised a hand to stop him. "Why haven't we named this mysterious female operative? Well, her real name is Sarah Hopewell, but don't ever let it cross your lips in public."

"Why haven't I met her yet? I like to know who the hell my life depends on."

"Oh, you'll meet her. As to why not yet—well, you know what an old fuss-and-feathers Allan can be. He's got these strict notions about professional conduct among his employees, you see, and—"

"And to bobtail all your mealymouthing, she's pretty as four aces and he's afraid I'll try to bed her?"

"She's pretty as *five* aces, Fargo, and you will try to bed her. I sure's hell would if I had your looks and confidence."

"Say, John, does this mean I'm spoken for?" Fargo barbed, and the other man flushed red.

"Damn it to hell, you're holding back something yourself," Fargo complained. "Give."

Fowler started and his eyes ran from Fargo's. "You're a sharp detective yourself, Fargo. All right, I am holding back something. But trust me, I *have* to. I'm not one for hunches,

Fargo, even when I have a strong one. I give you my word—when it's more than just a hunch, you'll be the first to know."

Fargo cursed mildly. "Seems to me that you and Pinkerton are trying to stuff the hog by way of its ass. I don't cotton to being part of a deal where everybody plays it so cagey. Pinkerton's got a third suspect he won't name, you've got a hunch you won't play, and me? Looks like I'm trying to screw a woman I don't even know."

Fowler's moon face looked suddenly despondent. "Hell, Fargo, it's not—"

"Never mind the ring-around-the-rosy. Is there *any* damn thing I'm allowed to know?"

"As a matter of fact, yeah. A hunch I *can* share. I got my eye on a down-at-the-heels shit-jobber named Kirby Doyle. He's not actually on the payroll at Adams Express, but he's paid pocket money to run errands and do light jobs for them. He's also sort of a night watchman for their wagon yard—sleeps in a little slope-off shed behind the building."

"Why is that useful to know? You got something on him?"

"Not yet," Fowler admitted. "But I've spent a good many years sizing up killers, and he's got that look. He's trying to pass himself off as a no-'count bummer, even a halfwit, but I've got an idea he's hell on two sticks. He's my responsibility since he's here in town, but I figure you should know how the wind sets."

"Interesting," Fargo said.

"What about this grudge Jack Parsons has against you? If the jealous asshole is trying to kill you, that could bollix up your plans to infiltrate the gang. Lattimer may rule the roost, but he'd play hell finding a cracksman as good as Parsons—he'd likely shit-can you if he's forced to a choice between you."

Fargo nodded and stood up, clapping his hat on. "I'm taking that bull by the horns right now."

Fargo was halfway to the door when he thought of something else and turned around. "I take it you know who Inge Johanson is?"

Fowler grinned. "Does a rag doll have a patched ass? Every red-blooded man in Saint Joe knows. Mister, *that's* silk."

"Yeah, well, according to Lily Reece her old man is making a serious play for Inge, and it sounds like she's a *very* expensive play-pretty. Could explain why Reece might want a lot of extra money pronto."

Fowler glanced at the toes of his shoes. "It's a thought, but she's stringing several men along."

"One of them being Hardiman Burke. So if I was you and Pinkerton I'd nose into that angle deeper. She doesn't strike me as the criminal type, so maybe Pinkerton should try to approach her, see if she knows anything useful."

"Good idea," Fowler said.

Fargo's eyes narrowed to slits. "Good idea? An obvious idea, too. Why didn't you tell me it's already been done? Ring around the goddamn rosy."

His face disgusted, Fargo walked out before Fowler could reply.

Fargo slipped the headstall over the Ovaro's ears and fastened the throat latch. Then he tossed on blanket, pad and saddle, cinched the girth and checked the latigos before he forked leather. The stallion was eager to stretch out the night kinks, and Fargo tightened the reins to control him.

"Easy, old warhorse," he said as he gigged the Ovaro toward the street. "We'll eat up some landscape when we get to the bluffs."

Fast riders were fined in Saint Joe so Fargo held the impatient stallion to an easy trot, slapping his glossy rump hard the moment they reached the stage road. Fargo let the stallion run hard until they were two miles south of Saint Joe, then cooled him out for the next half mile before veering off into the thick pine woods.

"Hallo, the camp!" he called out. "Fargo riding in!"

The trio greeted his arrival with varied reactions: Dog Man cynically amused, Lattimer wary, Parsons scowling.

"The hell you want?" Lattimer groused as Fargo lit down and tossed the reins forward. "I told you I'd send word when I wanted to talk at you."

Fargo nodded toward Parsons, who sat on a log whittling. "You best talk at that dumb yack. I'm about a cat whisker away from snuffing his wick."

Parsons's big, bluff face turned purple. "Don't be swingin' your eggs around here, Fargo. You costed me a jaw tooth yesterday. It ain't over, you son of a bitch."

"Then let's put paid to it now. I ain't the boy for by and by."

Parsons dropped his case knife and piece of wood, easing to his feet. "Go ahead, Fargo—skin it back, Mr. Gunologist. It's three on one, and even you ain't *that* fast."

"Leave me out of it," Dog Man said, grinning. "Just 'cause you're death on crazy redheads, Jack, and get your ass kicked in the street don't make it skin off *my* ass. Ain't none of them bitches worth a shinplaster."

Lattimer, squatting on his rowels and drinking coffee, looked asquint at Fargo. "Long-shanks, you may be the hero of the crapsheets, but *I'm* the biggest toad in this puddle. Savvy that?"

"I never thought otherwise. But your man Parsons is a dog off his leash."

"Stow it. You can't expect to prod my men and turn around and collect wages from me. Jack's a pain in the ass, all right, but he's the best cracksman I ever worked with. You *ain't* gonna burn him down, y'unnerstan'?"

Dog Man pitched in. "Christ, Jack, one night I watched that redheaded she-devil damn near peel the hide off you. A woman ever done me like that, she'd be looking up to see daisies. Hell, Fargo done you a favor by taking your place."

"Shut pan, you half-breed whoreson!" Parsons snapped.

"See how it is, Fargo?" Lattimer demanded. "I don't get it. The first time you was here, you was in a puffin' hurry to hop on some little calico in town. And then, the very next night, you got to prong Jack's whore? What, you gonna screw every female in Saint Joe and then start in on the sheep?"

Dog Man gave a harsh bark of laughter. Lattimer sent him a quelling stare.

"To me it's *all* squack," Lattimer resumed. "I druther fight over a cold biscuit than a piece of poon. But we can't expect to work together with you two always on the peck. A hound like you combs pussy hair out of his teeth every morning— you don't need to horn in where an ugly son of a bitch like Jack is gettin' his best."

This was all shaping up exactly as Fargo had hoped it would. He made his tone more reasonable.

"All right, so Parsons is the jealous type and he's got a pinecone lodged up his ass because I topped Lily Reece. But the big lummox tried to gun me down last night over something that piddling? I'll stand down, Jude, but I'm within my rights if I irrigate his guts right now."

Parsons took an angry step forward. "Fargo, you shit-cating liar! I been here in camp since yesterday afternoon."

That claim set Fargo back on his heels.

"I can vouch for him," Lattimer said.

"Don't look at me, chumley," Dog Man said. "I had a perfect chance to kill you when I got the drop on you last night."

Fargo nodded, genuinely baffled. "Yeah. Well, *some*body tried to kill me last night—or maybe Lily."

"That rich Whore of Babylon is dangerous meat, Fargo," Dog Man put in. "There could be a dozen jealous, pussy-whipped fools like Jack out there. You'd be smarter to get your package wrapped somewheres else."

Lattimer poured out the dregs of his coffee and stood up. He stared first at Fargo, then Parsons. "*Both* of you churn-brains lissenup. No more truck with Lily Reece, savvy? That croppy is six sorts of hell. Both of you will likely come down with the French pox."

Lattimer looked at Fargo now. "Trailsman, I'd sure-God like to have you along for this next job. Not only can I use a shootist like you, but we *will* need a good scout. This is our last heist, and we have to hightail it out of Missouri. We'll be sticking to rough country, and we got plenty of Pukes and Jayhawkers to slip past not to mention posses to outrun. But there'll be no more clash of stags, y'unnerstan'?"

"Understood. I'm just a mite curious, is all. Don't you have to clear me with the higher-ups?"

Lattimer's bone-button eyes bored into Fargo. "The higher-ups ain't none a your beeswax, *comprende*? *I'm* your boss."

Lattimer shifted his gaze to Parsons. "Katy Christ! I never seen the like in all my born days. Two men in line to make a king's ransom for a few days' work, but willing to piss it all away over a pert skirt. Fargo, I've decided on ten thousand for your share, and, Jack, you'll be gettin' more 'n that."

"Did I hear you right?" Fargo said. "Ten thousand?"

"Did I stutter? Men back east bust their humps twelve hours a day in them manufactories for one dollar a day. Chew on that, lover boy."

Fargo looked at Parsons. "Jack, I rode in here believing you tried to send me over the mountains last night. Now I know different. I owe you an apology."

"You owe me a goddamn, mother-ruttin' tooth, too," Parsons said in a sullen tone, and Fargo knew right then there was no way around it—eventually he'd have to kill this man.

9

Fargo spent his third night in Saint Joseph sleeping in a straw-cushioned stall next to the Ovaro. The arrangements suited him fine, but for strategic reasons he had decided to follow John Fowler's suggestion and move into the drab but inexpensive Ozark Hotel on River Street.

However, events on his fourth morning in town changed his mind for him.

Fargo had rolled out early and was surprised to find Septimus up and dressed, brewing coffee on the old Franklin stove in the tack room.

"Help yourself to the bear-sign," he greeted Fargo, pointing to a tin plate on a nearby trestle table. "Bought 'em fresh this morning."

Fargo thanked him and tied into one of the huge bear-paw-shaped doughnuts, wildly popular breakfast fare throughout the West. He washed it down with hot black coffee.

"What's got into you?" Fargo asked between bites. "Religion? Not only up with the birds, but sober as a Quaker."

"Oh, I had me a skinful last night," Septimus admitted. "Passed out early. When the fumes clear outta my skull, I'll commence to imbibin'. Drink is the work of the cursing classes."

Fargo chuckled at the pun. "Each man to his own gait. But I'm damned if I want to be controlled by the bottle."

Septimus surprised him. "That shows good mentality, Fargo. I wouldn't drink so goldang much iffen I was a more sociable cuss. But I just got no enthusiasm for the company of others. When a man's alone with his thoughts alla time, sometimes them thoughts get rough and ugly. A few swallers of who-shot-john smooths 'em out."

Fargo nodded. At times, too much solitude plagued even him, a man who usually sought the emptiest corner of the canyon by choice. But a young man at least had the pleasure of a willing woman now and then. Septimus seemed to pluck this thought from Fargo's head.

"Say, I ain't sloppin' over, Fargo, nor feelin' sorry for myself. Mister, I *seen* the elephant in my time. Spent three years making my beaver with the Taos Trappers. I been alla way down the King's Highway to Durango, Mexico, and fit Comanch in west Texas. My calves has gone to grass, mebbe, but my spine has still got all its stiff even iffen my pecker ain't."

"I'd gladly suffer a bad back," Fargo quipped, "to keep my snake biting. Say . . . mind if I borrow a rasp and a shoe-ing hammer?"

"Help yourself. Over on the bench."

Fargo had had an extra set of four new horseshoes made in Kansas City. He pulled them out of a saddle pannier, then led the Ovaro from his stall into the morning sunlight of the paddock. Septimus followed them outside carrying the tools.

"I seen them shoes on your stallion is a little worn," he said.

Fargo nodded, bending the Ovaro's rear nearside leg up to pry off the shoe. He inspected the foot—hoof, pastern and fetlock—carefully. "I heard this one clicking a little bit last time I rode out. It's working loose."

"All it takes is for a tiny crack to work its way up from the hoof into the coronet, and a horse pulls up lame."

Again Fargo nodded, interrupting his labors to take a good squint around. It had bothered him plenty when he believed Jack Parsons was trying to air him out; it bothered him even worse now that he had no clear idea exactly who was trying to kill him.

"Yeah," he replied absently to the old hostler. "Bad shoe-ing has lamed more horses than any other cause, I reckon."

Fargo recalled his visit yesterday with Fowler and the for-mer lawman's hunch. He began rasping the Ovaro's hoof smooth, preparing it for the new shoe.

"What do you know," he asked Septimus, "about a jasper named Kirby Doyle?"

Septimus, still munching bear-sign, gave Fargo a queer look. "What, that worthless hod carrier? The hell you care about him? He's got less get-up than a gourd vine."

"Maybe so, but I hear he works for Hardiman Burke at the express office."

At mention of the express office Septimus narrowed his eyes to slits, studying Fargo closely. "Hell, he just does odd jobs mostly for his keep. Lazy sumbitch who ties his hair off like an Injin—ain't worth spit. But he's harmless as a gopher snake."

"A gopher snake isn't so harmless if you're a gopher."

"That's too far north for me. Say, speakin' of the express office—how you doin' on that brag you made? You know, how you plan to wind Inge Johanson's clock for her?"

Fargo thumbed his hat back and gave the old man a rueful grin. "No progress to report yet. But hope is a waking dream."

"Hunh! A dream is the onliest way you'll ever trim her. May I be eternally damned iffen I can understand women. This Inge—why, she's already rolling in it! Got the best room at the Patee, the finest feathers in town, and here she is lettin' the likes of Burke and Mayor Reece court her. Hell, a gal that young and peart should want a young buck, not windbags and clothes dummies nearbout twice her age. Don't it beat the Dutch?"

Fargo was about to reply when, all of an instant, he realized what a lunkhead he'd been.

"I *am* a sorry son of a bitch," he muttered. "I missed it all along."

"How's 'at, bo?"

"I said you're right on the money, Septimus. I can't find any sign on a woman's breast, either."

Of course, Fargo told himself. Inge Johanson was actually Sarah Hopewell, Pinkerton's secret—and likely most effective—weapon. Plenty of beautiful women were gold diggers, all right, and many married a man's bankroll, not his looks. But this particular beautiful lass was charming two of the principal suspects on Pinkerton's short list—and hadn't Pinkerton and Fowler assured Fargo the mystery female operative was some pumpkins?

The apparent wealth—Pinkerton was known for pulling out all the stops on an important case. Fargo had to forgive him for his fear that the Trailsman wouldn't be able to resist this woman, for in truth he couldn't and wouldn't even try.

Fargo finished rasping the hoof and reached for a horse-shoe nail, still grinning at the turn this trail had suddenly taken. He heard the Ovaro snuffle and glanced up just in time to see the stallion's ears prick forward.

"Septimus!" he shouted. "Kiss the dirt *now*!"

He cursed when the old man just stood there with a blank face. Fargo leaped at him and tackled him, a move that likely saved Fargo's life if not the old man's. Only a heartbeat after he leaped, a gunshot cracked loudly above the bustle of the street.

A gentle strawberry roan, one of Septimus's for-hire horses, had been drinking at the long stone water trough in the paddock. Fargo saw a dust puff rise from the roan's flank only an eyeblink before its front knees buckled. Crying piteously, the horse collapsed, its sides heaving like a bellows.

Septimus loosed a bray of rage. "Great jumpin' Judas! Some son of a whore just kilt Comet!"

"Stay down, you fool!" Fargo snapped.

He had already filled his hand with blue steel, but the street was bustling and he spotted no one who seemed a likely target. Fargo waited a minute before he pushed to his feet, giving the ashen-faced liveryman a hand up.

A quick inspection of Comet revealed an ugly, puckered wound where the bullet had penetrated a lung. Pink froth bubbled from the animal's nostrils. Gritting his teeth to steel himself for the awful task, Fargo put the roan out of its misery with one clean shot.

Septimus stared at the dead horse in confusion. "By the horn spoons! Why would anybody want to kill my horse?"

"Your horse wasn't the target," Fargo said. "And neither were you. I was standing right in front of Comet when I jumped to tackle you."

The old man's tired, rheumy eyes shifted to Fargo. "Ahuh. Trouble *is* the street you live on, hey?"

Septimus expelled a long, weary sigh. "Well, there's a

knacker one street over. He'll haul the carcass out for me iffen I let him have the meat."

"You'll be paid the full value of that horse," Fargo promised, realizing it could easily have been the Ovaro that went down. "And I'll get the hell out of here today."

Septimus pulled at the gray scruff on his chin. "Just tell me this much, Fargo—arc you workin' *for* the law or agin it?"

"I'm no scrubbed angel, but I've never worked against it in my life—and I'm not now."

Septimus nodded. "That's good enough for me. You just stay here as long as you've a need to. I wa'n born in the woods to be scairt by an owl. I'll be hog-tied and earmarked afore I'll run a good man out just on account some chicken-pluckin' curly wolves is after him. Life's hard 'nuff for a man what takes a stand in lawless country."

Fargo gazed at the dead horse and realized—if he did move to the Ozark, the Ovaro would spend long stretches at the livery unprotected. Whoever had tried to kill him just now almost certainly worked for the syndicate—and they were surely smart enough to know that Skye Fargo would be at a distinct disadvantage without the Ovaro.

"You got a piece?" he asked Septimus.

"A Colt Army in the tack room. Feller left it in payment. It's a mite dinged up, but it barks."

"A gun's no use if it isn't in easy reach," Fargo said. "Stick it in your belt. Since it's all right with you, I will stay on here for a bit—and I'm beholden, old-timer."

"Ahh . . . how many old farts can brag how they sided the Trailsman in a scrape?"

"Stall my stallion, wouldja? I won't be gone long."

"Where you headed?" Septimus called out to his back.

"Just playing a hunch," Fargo replied.

The Adams Freighting and Express Company was located on Jules Street two blocks east of the courthouse. A brick furnace had recently been built in Saint Joe, and the express office was one of the new redbrick buildings sprouting up.

Fargo approached from the opposite side of the street, taking advantage of the motley flow of humanity and conveyances to hide his presence. A large wagon yard lay adjacent to the office, currently occupied by a huge Owensboro freight wagon and a thorough-braced Concord swift wagon. Fargo spotted a man greasing the hubs of the Concord and scrutinized him closely.

His hair fit Septimus's description: long and parted in the middle, tied off in back with a rawhide whang. He wore dirty white sailcloth trousers and a gray homespun shirt filthy as a sop rag. He carried no weapon in plain view.

Fargo was about to step into the street but checked himself when the front door of the express office opened and Hardiman Burke stepped outside with Inge Johanson on his arm.

Again Fargo marveled at the striking figure she cut. Her velvet and lace dress was not ridiculously ballooned out by the currently fashionable crinoline cage and showed her graceful sweeps and curves to good advantage without making her look "fast."

Although he had no proof, Fargo was convinced she was Pinkerton's secret operative. The master crime fighter was known for employing some real beauties, and Fargo figured that if she was spending so much time with Burke she must have good reasons.

Once again Burke was tailored to the image of frontier success, this time in a vermillion ranch suit with a fancy gold watch chain looping across the silk vest. Looking at him, Fargo felt a familiar contempt. He had learned long ago that a very small, elite group of men controlled the mass of humanity through fraud and violence, raping the continent and pilfering the public coffers.

That didn't mean, however, Fargo reminded himself, that Hardiman Burke was the mastermind of a criminal gang.

He watched them bear east on Jules Street, on foot, and make the jog onto Frederick Street. Curious, remaining on the opposite side of the street, Fargo followed them.

They stopped in front of the city's premier eatery, the Hathaway House, owned by the same railroad baron who built the Patee. A minute later a one-seat runabout pulled by a handsome bay pulled up beside the couple. Fargo watched a distinguished-looking army officer, silver-haired and dapper, light down and join them. A Chinese worker in a floppy blue blouse and long pigtail stepped out of the eatery and drove the runabout to a lot behind the Hathaway House.

Fargo, brow wrinkled in speculation, watched the trio enter the eating house. He recalled Pinkerton's reticence on the subject of the third suspect: *I'm not yet ready to name him. I'm more disposed to respect him and give him the benefit of the doubt.*

Fargo was unable to see the officer's shoulder epaulets at this distance, but his age and bearing—and the private runabout—suggest a high rank. Could this be suspect number three? Any gold shipment intended for the U.S. Treasury would certainly involve the army.

Fargo reversed his dust back toward the express office. The man he figured to be Kirby Doyle was still greasing hubs, and clearly setting no speed record. Dodging wagon traffic, Fargo ambled across the street.

"Howdy," he greeted the other man in a hail-fellow voice, affecting a hayseed drawl.

Doyle's flat gunmetal eyes shifted reluctantly toward the speaker. Fargo detected a split second of surprised recognition before the glance slid away again.

"That sure is a fine-looking rig," Fargo enthused. "Four-in-hand, ain't it?"

Fargo knew that Western coaches, because of terrain and distances, were pulled by at least six horses. But Doyle didn't bother to enlighten him as he smeared grease on the rear offside hub.

"Yes, indeed," Fargo rambled on. "I've never had the pleasure of riding in a by-God Concord, but I hear that a swift wagon with a good team can cut dirt at nine miles per hour. Is that straight goods?"

Doyle's voice, when he finally replied, was as flat as his eyes. "Couldn't tell you. I only work on 'em."

Fargo glanced inside the coach. "Yessir, this is a *fine* rig. Upholstered with leather, and just look at them fancy side curtains."

Doyle, kneeling beside the wheel, pointedly ignored Fargo. But the Trailsman could see how the man's initial surprise was transforming into irritation—exactly what Fargo wanted.

"I been told the best seat in a coach is the first one behind the driver—only half the bumps. And a knight of the ribbons—that's a stagecoach driver—told me once that if a team runs away, it's best to sit still and take your chances. He says nine times out of ten, you'll get hurt if you jump. You—"

"Turn off the goddamn tap!"

Doyle set his grease pail down and rose to his feet. He was only an inch shy of Fargo's six-foot frame. "You must have a brick in your hat."

"Hell, I'm not drunk. I just like these Concord rigs."

"I don't give a continental damn *what* you like. Why'n't you just fade?"

John Fowler's instincts were right, Fargo decided. Something about this "roustabout" just wouldn't tally. The cold stare, the hard, emotionless manner, the impression that he was only a hairsbreadth from explosive violence. . . . He deliberately wore no gun, but Fargo was convinced he had one less than a half hour ago, notched squarely on the Trailsman.

Now Fargo played his hole card. "Who's paying you to kill me, Doyle? It can't be Lattimer—his bunch had their chance to croak me."

Knocked off-kilter by the sudden bluntness, Doyle nervously fingered the heavy brass studding on his belt. "You're crazy as a shite-poke."

"I asked you a question, b'hoy. Who talked you into signing your own goddamn death warrant?"

"Mister, I don't even own a gun. You been misinformed. I just work hard for a living and mind my own business."

"You're a liar, Doyle—a cowardly, back-shooting liar. I know what a workingman's hands look like. You're just a soft-handed bastard who hires out to cowards unwilling to do their own killing."

"Now *if* that was true, you'd be mighty damn stupid to say it to my face, huh?"

"Only if you were man enough to do it—and if I intended to let you live."

"So you're saying you mean to kill me?"

"I ain't saying I mean to—I'm saying I will. You opened the ball when you killed that horse instead of me, now the last dance is mine. But I like to let a man know it's coming

68

so he can think about it—let it gnaw on him. It's anticipation that adds savor to life."

"Hell, you got no proof I tried to kill you."

"The proof," Fargo said in a low, resolute voice, "is *you*. The way you're acting right now and the greasy, four-flushing, snake-eyed look of you. But just to put a legal ribbon on it, I *will* make sure I have the proof before I shoot you low in the belly and leave you screaming in the dirt, hellfire burning in your guts. And I'll make sure I find out which one of the big bugs is paying you, too. Think about it, shit heel, think long and hard. You pulled down the thunder when you tried to kill Skye Fargo."

This promissory spiel clearly left Doyle rattled. But he quickly recovered and set his thin-lipped mouth hard. "Man's got him a mouth like yours, maybe somebody'll fix his flint—fix it real good. The worm always turns."

"Funny you should mention worms," Fargo replied just before he walked off. "Because it won't be long before they're dining on your eyeballs."

10

Fargo spent the rest of that morning, and the first part of the afternoon, continuing to range over the surrounding terrain, scouting and making the valuable "mind maps" that had often pulled his bacon out of the fire. He also wanted the Ovaro familiar with the area, knowing any horse was most reliable on familiar ground.

"That-air Uncle Pete a yours sent word agin," Septimus greeted him when Fargo returned to the livery. "Wants to see you after supper."

Fargo nodded as he pulled his saddle and checked the Ovaro for galls. "I see that knacker hauled your dead roan off."

"Ahuh. I'll let your *uncle* off light, Fargo. A hunnert dollars will square it. Comet was worth twice that, but I ain't one to cry roast beef the minute I see mustard."

"It's a fair price. Uncle Pete is a tight-fisted piker, but I'll shake it out of him."

Fargo visited a gun shop in the heart of town and purchased a hundred-count box of shells for his Colt, making sure it was factory ammo and not hand-crimped. Neither type was completely reliable, but lately hand-crimped shells with dangerously light powder loads had flooded the market. Factory ammo too often failed to prime, but Fargo was damned if he was going to count on bullets with thirty-grain loads.

He killed more time wandering around Saint Joseph, seeing if Kirby Doyle or any other graveyard rat was feeling froggy enough to jump him. After buying a sack of horehound candy from a train butch at the railroad station, Fargo enjoyed a leisurely supper of ice-cold beer and chipped beef on biscuits at the Hog's Breath.

Reasonably certain no one had followed him in, Fargo ducked into the cellar of the Hog's Breath and followed the Indian tunnel to the alley next to Pinkerton's office on Charles Street. He rapped out the signal on the rear door and was bade enter.

Pinkerton sat at his Texas-size desk, knocking the dottle out of his meerschaum. John Fowler leaned against a side wall covered with wanted dodgers, his face sly and expectant as he watched Fargo step inside.

And the reason for Fowler's sly expectation sat demurely in a cane-bottom chair beside Pinkerton, breathtakingly beautiful in a black sateen dress and pearl-button shoes.

"Skye Fargo," Pinkerton began the amenities, "I'd like you to meet—"

"Charmed to finally meet you, Miss Hopewell." Fargo cut him off. "I observed you at your duties earlier today and almost wished I was a criminal."

Pinkerton placed his pipe on the desk, his face astounded. "So John spilled the beans?"

"He didn't need to. I finally developed a remarkable grasp for the obvious. How could a female Pinkerton operative have found time to close-herd Reece, Burke and maybe even an army officer with the lovely Inge Johanson in the mix? Only if the two ladies were one and the same."

"Army officer, eh?" Pinkerton said as Fargo dropped into a chair opposite the belle femme. "You know, Skye, it's not your job to worry overly much about anyone in town."

"Oh, Mr. Fargo is a busy man indeed," Sarah Hopewell spoke up with a mischievous sparkle in those alluring blue eyes. "John mentioned your visit to Lily Reece. That must have been quite . . . interesting. Have your welts healed yet? A solution of gentian root and yarrow paste might be quite soothing."

Fowler coughed, then covered a smirk with his hand. Even the stern, no-nonsense Pinkerton let his lips quirk into a brief smile.

Fargo, unperturbed, looked her bluntly in the eyes. "One thing I did *not* taste during that visit was rawhide. And Miss Reece seemed tame enough when I left."

"Tame . . . or merely disappointed?"

This time Fowler chortled openly. Pinkerton cleared his throat. "This is a *business* meeting, remember?"

"She fired the first salvo," Fargo remarked.

"Never mind. Fargo, what was this incident earlier at the livery? According to one of John's sources, someone tried to kill you?"

"Not someone," Fargo corrected him, still openly admiring his blond associate. "A sage rat named Kirby Doyle."

"Doyle!" Sarah exclaimed. "You can't be serious?"

"Serious as a smallpox blanket," Fargo assured her.

"I *knew* it," Fowler said. "He's a stone-cold killer."

Pinkerton looked miffed. "Evidently I'm the only one present who's never heard of Kirby Doyle. Would any of my *employees* care to enlighten me?"

"I find Mr. Fargo's assertion somewhat amusing," Sarah said. "Kirby Doyle doesn't even carry a weapon. I believe he's what they term a roustabout. He performs menial tasks for Adams Express, and while I admit I don't know him, I have observed him. He seems a bit of a simpleton."

"The cowl doesn't make the monk," Fargo said. "I don't have the proof, but I confronted him and I'm convinced—he's on somebody's secret payroll and he wasn't hired to fork fodder."

Pinkerton said, "Fargo, didn't you say you're convinced Lattimer could have killed you already—that, since he didn't, he must want you in the gang?"

Fargo placed his hat on his knee and bobbed his head.

"Then your claim makes no sense. Surely whoever leads the syndicate would be in control of decisions as to whomever Lattimer hires. Why should they work at cross purposes?"

"That one's got me treed," Fargo admitted.

Pinkerton frowned. "And yet you confronted him, and on the basis of a mere hunch?"

"*Two* hunches," Fowler put in. "I'm the one who warned Skye about him. Both of us have been bouncing criminal scum-suckers around long enough to recognize the type."

Pinkerton gave that a nod. "I'll grant that much. But I must warn both of you—again—that we don't have the latitude of Texas Rangers. The Pinkerton Agency requires evidence, as would any criminal prosecution resulting from our involvement."

"That sweet-lavender lawing may work back in Boston," Fargo said. "But on the frontier most men are just a face with a name—one that changes at the drop of a hat. All due respect, Miss Hopewell, but you're wrong—this Kirby Doyle may *look* like just another wage slave with pants gone through at the knees. But he's poison mean and he tried to kill me. And he was following orders when he did it."

"Fargo," Pinkerton admonished in a lecturing tone, "you're good at pulping a man's lips against his teeth. But you can't smash your way to every solution. Sarah has been on this case since the investigation began, and she understands the complexities involved."

The comely blonde smiled sweetly at Fargo. "Oh, I suspect Mr. Fargo understands subtlety, all right, Allan. He just doesn't let it get in his way. No doubt he can't really help it—just as a fish doesn't know it's wet, our famous Trailsman doesn't realize he's crude. After all, he dresses in animal skins like our ancient forebearers."

Fargo felt his lips tugging into a grin. "Straight ahead and keep up the strut, that's me. Girl, you're good. I mean *good*. This syndicate hasn't got a snowball's chance."

"Never mind personalities," Pinkerton said, reigning over all of this with patrician reserve. That cool aplomb was shattered, however, by Fargo's next comment.

"Allan, I need a hundred dollars before I leave here."

Pinkerton's jaw slacked open. "You need—? I will *not* cover your gambling debts!"

"Simmer down." Fargo explained about the dead horse. "You told me, when I hired on, that you'd cover any legitimate expenses caused by my working for you. Septimus Perkins is on the hook for one dead horse, and *I* sure's hell don't have the money to give him."

Pinkerton was a miser but a scrupulous one. His face pained, he removed a metal box from his desk and counted out five double-eagle gold pieces. "I want an invoice," he groused as Fargo pocketed the money. "Next time, stand clear of the horses."

Pinkerton beamed at his female operative. "Now, to the main point of this meeting. Thanks to Sarah's—"

"I *do* wish all three of you would get in the habit of calling me—even thinking about me—as Inge," she protested. "One slip of the tongue at the wrong time could be devastating."

"Quite so, my dear. Thanks to Inge's good work, we have new information that forces me to add the name of Colonel Ambrose Meriwether to our list of suspects. John, you already know who he is. Fargo, is that name familiar to you?"

Fargo shook his head. "I know, or know of, most of the field commanders with that rank."

"Meriwether is a Beacon Hill Bostonian who's always been a featherbed soldier. For the past several years he's been an investigator with the War Department's Financial Security Division. Two years ago he was himself investigated for possible involvement in several military payroll heists at Fort Union. But he was eventually cleared of all charges and allowed to retain his present position."

"Sure," Fargo put in. "I read something about it in *Police Gazette*."

"Yes, but now it appears he *may* either be in cahoots with the mastermind of our syndicate or be the brains behind it himself. Inge . . . would you care to elaborate?"

"Colonel Meriwether is a very polished gentleman with a wife and three children back in Maryland. He rents a nice cottage on Enterprise Street only a few blocks from Mayor Reece's home"—she interrupted herself to again smile sweetly at Fargo—"which of course you already know about."

"I haven't seen any master bedrooms yet," Fargo fired back pointedly, and Inge bristled like a feist.

"*Please*, you two." Pinkerton interceded. "Inge, no side commentaries. Fargo, pretend you have manners."

She gave Fargo one last go-to-hell look before resuming. "Today I managed to get the colonel and Hardiman Burke together with me for breakfast at the Hathaway House. I assumed they are rivals for my attention, and perhaps they are. But while I was studying the menu, I saw Meriwether surreptitiously pass an envelope to Burke."

"And I've seen Meriwether and Josiah Reece gambling into the wee hours." Fowler waded in.

"Which might suggest," Pinkerton said, "that at least two of them, and possibly all three, run the syndicate. Colonel Meriwether is privy to every aspect of the gold shipments: time, route, security. He can also help sidetrack any investigations."

His eyes cut to Fowler. "He was acquitted two years ago, John, and we *won't* assume any guilt on his part. But perhaps, after all, it would be wise for you to employ your barkey and search his home while Inge keeps him occupied without?"

"You might have better luck," Fargo insisted, "searching that shack behind the express office where Doyle holes up. One thing I'd wager you'll find is a well-notched shooter in an oiled holster."

"And if me and Fargo are right about him," Fowler said, "we can use . . . persuasive means to find out who runs him."

Pinkerton pulled at his beard, mulling it. "Well, as long as I'm authorizing warrantless searches, the task of searching Doyle's shack will fall to you, Skye."

"Yes," Inge tossed in, "that red bandanna you wear at your throat must tug up easily into a mask."

"Makes a damn fine gag, too," Fargo warned. But he added a moment later: "Sar—I mean, Inge—Allan says Josiah Reece is on his list, too. But I've yet to see the man, and there's been little said about him here. His daughter pretty much admitted he's a scoundrel, but she didn't chew it very fine."

"So far I've learned very few specifics. But his greed for money is extraordinary. He told me once that a man who knows exactly how much money he has is not yet wealthy. Hardiman Burke, in contrast, talks less about money and more about his political ambitions."

"Which are best realized," Pinkerton reminded the trio, "with plenty of money."

"Well, *both* of them have a real facility with clichés," Inge said. "They should thrive in politics. Neither one of them really makes a solid point—they just skirmish around the edges. Colonel Meriwether, in contrast, is a West Point man and a plain but intelligent speaker. He is also, however, quite guarded at times, which leads me to wonder if he needs to be."

"Just curious," Fargo interrupted, still smarting from her previous insults. "Which one of the three has tried hardest to bed you—assuming that requires an effort?"

"*Damn* you, Fargo!" Pinkerton exploded, but Inge coolly stopped him with a raised hand.

"It may disappoint your salacious fantasies, Mr. Fargo," she replied calmly, "but unlike you, all three men consider me a respectable woman. Thus, they likely have mistresses on the side to satisfy their carnal appetites. Reece and Burke, one a widower, the other a bachelor, are competing to get me to the altar."

"Yeah? Well, Meriwether is married—what's in it for the colonel?"

"The companionship of a beautiful, cultured woman."

"That still leaves one question."

"That being . . . ?"

"What about *your* carnal appetites?"

"Fargo, you scoundrel!" Pinkerton boomed out.

Fargo gave him a harsh bark of laughter. "No need to have a hissy fit, detective man. It's obvious you and Fowler have got a case for her, and who can blame you? She plays men like pianos. Me, I don't fall in love with women."

Now he shifted his gaze to Inge. "I just give them what they want."

"That's easy enough," she shot back casually, "with women who want very little. Toss a beggar a dollar and he's rich."

She rose gracefully and Pinkerton shot to his feet. "John, if you'll kindly escort me to my hotel . . ."

She's no dumb frail, Fargo was forced to admit, feeling the sting of this fresh insult. After the two had left, Fargo looked at Pinkerton. "Go ahead, boss—time to talk like a book. Make your point."

"Why bother? The one on your head just beat me to it. Fargo, you had no call to insult her that way."

Fargo stood up and clapped his hat on, then flashed strong white teeth through his beard. "She sent out the first soldier—

I only sent out the second. Besides, you got a lot to learn about beautiful women. She's a scrapper and she loved every minute of it, and now I'm in her mind—in it real good. And it's a mighty short step from the mind to the mattress."

Night had just begun to drag her indigo burial shroud across the sky when Fargo left Pinkerton's office. He had intended to return to the livery and turn in early. But one block south of Charles Street he spotted a familiar long-haired figure slouching under the anemic halo of a streetlight.

Kirby Doyle. Fargo let him get a half block farther, then fell in step behind him.

Doyle sauntered along in the easy way of men who live in towns and take their sights for granted. Fargo didn't see a gun or knife on him, a fact that seemed a mite queer in this frontier heller where weapons vastly outnumbered people. Either there was a hideout weapon tucked into one of his boots, or this was all a sham—a perfect ploy for a hired killer who didn't want his profession known.

Doyle headed for River Street with its section of seedy barrelhouse joints frequented by boatmen and the rowdier elements of Saint Joseph. There was always the outside chance, Fargo told himself, that Doyle might meet with one of the Lattimer bunch. But that seemed unlikely and Fargo still suspected Doyle was "private stock," working for an individual with an agenda at odds with the syndicate.

His quarry ducked into a ramshackle building billing itself as COOTER BROWN'S GROG SHOP. A tout no older than twelve worked the street out front, drumming up business for the groggery.

"Finest young ladies in Saint Joe, gents, none with the dripping disease! Huzzah! Stout porter, threepenny ale, the only honest faro game in town. Huzzah, huzzah!"

Fargo stepped in a minute behind Doyle and was enveloped in a blue, shifting cloud of tobacco smoke. The stale reek of unwashed masculinity and cheap, cloying perfume assaulted his nostrils.

"H'ar now, clear the door, Dan'l Boone!" a gravelly voice growled behind Fargo, who had paused to look for Doyle. "Gangway or I'll baste your bacon!"

77

Fargo turned around to confront a barrel-chested, red-faced brute wearing the butternut-dyed cloth of a Puke. He carried a Sharps .50 and a magazine pistol protruded from his sash.

"I've been called far worse than Dan'l Boone," Fargo replied, his voice raised to counter the teeming ruckus within. "The real story here is that a bald-headed, pin-dick baboon can speak."

By now the bully had a better view of this tall, broad-shouldered, rock-jawed frontiersman who smiled with his lips only.

"P'r'aps I was out of line, Dan'l," he reconsidered, swinging wide around Fargo.

Fargo's eyes swept the joint, which reminded him of the roach-infested holes he'd seen in San Francisco's Barbary Coast and New Orleans's Smoky Row. A pretty but coarse-mannered faro dealer sat in a half circle of bettors while a case tender with a huge carbuncle on his neck called out each card like a circus barker.

A few battered billiard tables were scattered about, sporting bullet holes and patched felts. Several dime-a-dance girls wearing feather boas were working the customers, rubbing up against them to get them primed for the soiled doves.

A bouncer with brass knuckle-dusters wrapped around his right hand noticed that Fargo was just looking around.

"This is not Freeman's Quay, mate!" he warned. "We have whiskey, women and bucking the tiger! Roust out your gelt or emigrate."

Fargo flipped him a Liberty half dollar and made a fast friend. Just then he spotted Kirby Doyle at the bar. While most of the patrons around him nursed mugs of warm beer, Doyle purchased three shots of top-shelf whiskey in rapid succession. Then Fargo watched him buy a whorehouse chit from the bar dog and head up the stairs at the end of the bar.

A topside chit, not a token for the crib girls out back at one-third the price. For a "roustabout" living on grub wages, Kirby Doyle had some extravagant habits. The real stumper, Fargo thought as he gratefully headed outside into the cool night air, was *who* was financing those habits.

Well, he had Pinkerton's say-so to search Doyle's shack.

Fargo debated doing it right then, but most men spent less than two minutes on a whore, and he had no idea when the man would head back to his digs. Fargo decided to wait until the next time he saw Doyle heading out to cut the wolf loose.

He headed across town for the livery, recalling Doyle's not-so-veiled threat from earlier today: "Man's got him a mouth like yours, maybe somebody'll fix his flint—fix it real good. The worm always turns."

11

The Trailsman rolled out of the blanket, on his fifth day in Saint Joe, with his senses alert and his hand filled—the front doors had groaned open, and he half hoped to find Kirby Doyle cat-footing toward his stall.

Instead, he encountered a gangly, ashen-faced message runner wearing the red-billed cap of his profession. The kid was barely sixteen and stared wide-eyed at the Colt staring back at him.

"Don't shoot, mister. I got a message for a tall fellow wearing buckskins—I reckon that's you."

Fargo grinned and leathered his shooter. "Sorry, son. What's the word?"

"Some gent with a scarred-up face says you're to ride out to his camp 'quicker 'n scat.' That's all he said."

So Lattimer didn't want to be seen around Skye Fargo in town? That could just be routine caution, Fargo figured, or maybe a sign that a heist was imminent.

Fargo flipped the kid two bits and rigged the Ovaro, reluctantly deciding to forgo Katy's culinary prowess. He stepped up and over and rode out, Septimus still snoring with a racket like the mating call of a bull moose.

The sun was barely an hour over the eastern flats when Fargo hailed the outlaw camp and rode in.

Dog Man, squatting over a cooking fire, was the only one who bothered to greet him. "Stoked your belly yet? Got some fried pork left."

Fargo swung down and tossed the reins forward, glancing at the congealed mess in the frying pan. "No, thanks. That hog's seen better days."

"Fuck him, Dog Man," Parsons spat out around a mouthful of food. "He ain't no guest of honor."

Lattimer, squatting on his rowels and blowing on his coffee, glanced at Parsons with his bone-chip eyes. "Don't start it, Jack. I sent for Fargo."

"So wha'd'ya want, jewels in paradise? I got no use for him."

Dog Man flipped the meat in the sizzling grease, then looked at Fargo and winked. "Old Jack, he's what you call out of sorts. Seems he's wantin' that crazy redhead somethin' fierce since Jude ordered him to steer clear of her."

"He ordered Fargo to steer clear, too," Parsons snapped. "And I'll just bet a big one he is!"

"Fargo can shake the bushes and get all the poon he wants," Dog Man roweled his partner. "You're the one stuck skinning the cat."

Parsons's big bluff face twisted into a scowl. "I ain't in no funnin' mood, 'breed. That leather ear a yours would puke a buzzard off a gut wagon."

Fargo noticed Parsons was having trouble chewing the tough meat—no doubt because he'd lost his last good jaw tooth to Fargo's hard right fist.

"*Both* you bitches pipe down," Lattimer growled in his gravelly voice. "It's high time somebody read to you from the book, and *I'm* your goddamn preacher!"

His dead eyes slanted toward Fargo. "I told you I was keeping an eye on you in town. I'm told you like to drop outta sight now and then. What's that all about?"

"Survival. There's a reason why I generally fight shy of settlements," Fargo replied. "I've made my share of enemies over the years, and towns give them the best chance of popping me over. I see no reason to parade the fact I'm there."

Lattimer only grunted and slurped his coffee.

"Matter fact," Fargo added, watching him closely, "I been shot at twice now."

Lattimer looked a little more interested. "Twice? I knew about the one at the whore's house on Enterprise Street. When was the second?"

"Yesterday at the livery."

"Any idea who it was?"

"I'd bet my horse it's Kirby Doyle."

The look of blank surprise on Lattimer's face, Fargo decided, could be genuine or just good acting.

"Doyle?" Parsons repeated. "That's a lulu! Fargo, have you been grazin' locoweed? That shit-for-brains couldn't locate his own ass at high noon in a hall of mirrors."

"What proof you got?" Lattimer demanded.

"Nothing you can poke into a parfleche. Mainly just a hunch."

That seemed to set Lattimer thinking. Fargo got the impression these jackals knew damn well that Doyle was dangerous. But Lattimer seemed taken aback that he might have tried to kill Fargo.

"That knot-headed son of a bitch don't even own a weapon," Parsons scoffed. "The hell, Fargo? Coming in here blowing smoke up our ass . . . 'pears to me the big newspaper hero is gettin' a mite spooky on us."

"You know, Jack," Fargo said in his deceptively amiable manner, "I wouldn't piss in your ear if your brains were on fire. But I'm willing to overlook a few insults in the interest of financial gain. Unfortunately, it appears that you're aiming to settle some scores."

All three men were suddenly quiet and still. Nobody missed it when Fargo knocked the riding thong off the hammer of his Colt.

"Put it away from your mind, Fargo," Lattimer said. "It's true he's been prodding you, but we need the mouthy pup. He's the best cracksman I ever worked with. Dog Man will bear me out on that."

"I ain't hiding behind your skirts, Jude," Parsons blustered. "You two seen me knock Big Bat Landry out from under his hat in a draw-shoot. Hell, *this* jackass is scairt of Kirby Doyle. 'Pears to me like maybe he's got a liver problem. You know . . . yellow?"

Dog Man laughed so hard he had to cough his food back up. "Yellow? Jack, that's mite onspiritual of you. You're a fair hand with a barking iron, but that old boy standing over there is twice the man you are on his worst day. You pull down on him and you're trap bait."

"Lattimer," Fargo said impatiently, "is this why you dragged me out here? For a pissing contest with Jacky boy?"

"Not hardly. Fargo, I ain't at liberty to give partic'lars. But the last job is shaping up, and we need to scratch some plans out in the dirt."

Fargo felt a twinge of unease. Pinkerton's big idea was to hobble the syndicate from the top down—if this heist was coming up too damn soon, these three owlhoots would have to be stopped. And there was a good chance even they didn't know all the names involved.

"Glad to hear it," Fargo said. "There's no glory in peace."

"Like I said, we'll be cutting loose after this next job, and the four of us will be lighting a shuck for Mexico. You're s'posed to be the best tracker, scout and trailblazer in Zeb Pike country. So once we point our bridles south, *you'll* be calling the shots until we're south of the border."

"God*damn* it, Jude!" Parsons exploded. "Calling the shots? Him screwin' your sister ain't no kind of reference! I'm still dead set against dealing him in."

"Yeah? Well, him screwin' your crazy redhead whore ain't no reason to deal him *out*, neither. Tell me, are you dead set against living, too? Fargo is the boy who's gonna get us to Mexico. So far our clover's been deep, but none of us has got any trailcraft, and without him we'll just be sticking our heads in a noose."

Dog Man belched. "'At's right, Jack. We're gonna be guests of honor at the biggest damn strangulation jig since they lynched the Labun gang over at Lead Hill."

"Damn straight," Lattimer pitched back in. He spilled the dregs of his coffee and scoured the cup with a handful of grass. "They're gonna have redskin trackers dogging us, and thanks to the telegraph there'll be posses on our six all the way."

He looked at Fargo again. "You're the big scout and tracker—I wanna know some a your thoughts on how we get to Mexico alive."

"I been cogitating on that. First of all, right after the heist we all split up. It's harder to find and follow four separate trails, all made by one rider, than one big trail made by four."

"Nix on that." Lattimer cut in. "We'll each be hauling a

quarter of our share of the bullion, but we can't all scatter to hellangone. I made a deal with a jasper down in Galveston to buy the gold from us at eighty percent value. He *won't* dicker—it's all the gold or none. If even one of us gets killed or captured, the whole damn shivaree falls apart."

"Besides," Dog Man put in, "we're all dead shots, and four of us can toss more lead than one."

"Yeah, and just why is Fargo so consarn eager to split us?" Parsons demanded. "Maybe so he can hightail it to the law and spill the beans on us."

"Why'n't you put a tune to it, asshole?" Fargo said. "I could've done that by now. All I meant was, split up at first—just long enough to throw them off our trail."

"Nix," Lattimer repeated. "You dang well better have a few good fox plays, or you'll buy the farm bull and all."

"Well, if we can't raise the bridge, we'll lower the river. Do you at least agree that we should ride nights and hole up days?"

"With you as our trail honcho, sure."

"Indian trackers won't work after dark, and besides, the nights have got a snap to them and we can push the horses harder."

"Hell," Dog Man said, "I can figure that out. This all you got?"

Fargo grinned. "Steady, b'hoy, I'll spell it out. For one thing, each man is going to carry several sets of horseshoes with him, all forged at a different smithy. No two sets—even brand new—have the same forge marks or leave the same prints. We'll switch out on the fly. Indian trackers depend on consistent marks, nicks, ridge lines and chips in a print."

"That's more like it," Lattimer approved, and even the surly Jack Parsons was listening closely now.

"Once we get south of the Indian Territory," Fargo went on, "we can stick close to cattle trails and buffalo runs. Even a pure-quill featherhead plays hell picking out riders in the chewed-up mess made by cattle and buff. Each man is also going to have rawhide patches we can tie over the horses' hoofs. That won't help over soft ground, but on hardpan it almost eliminates any trail."

"Sweet," Dog Man said. "Now you're whistlin', Fargo."

"But if all else fails," Fargo resumed, "there's a simple trick that can shake a posse quick: We nail our horseshoes on backwards. At least for a time that'll send a posse in the opposite direction we're riding in."

The other three men glanced at each other, unsure if Fargo was pulling their legs.

"Stretching the blanket a mite, ain't you?" Lattimer said.

"Straight goods," Fargo insisted. "We can't keep it up long because of the risk of laming a horse. And they'll eventually twig the game when they take the time to notice the prints aren't spaced at the right distance from each other. But it usually works long enough to open out a good lead. I threw a Yaqui tracker off my spoor that way down in Sonora."

"I'll be goddamn," Lattimer said. "Fargo, sounds like you're a good man to take along, all right. But I'm worried about cover, too. There's plenty of open country south of Red River."

"There's an art to taking cover where there doesn't seem to be any. Blackjack, deadfalls, gulches—hell, in a pinch even a quick sand wallow will put a horse below the horizon once you wrestle it down. There's always cover."

"I see you *have* put a mind to it," Lattimer said grudgingly. "Now if—"

Fargo gripped his arm to cut him off. "Look at my horse," he said tersely.

All three men did. The Ovaro had been cutting grass at the edge of the little clearing. But now he stood with his neck craned toward the tree cover, ears pricked forward.

"Somebody's coming in," Fargo said just loud enough to be heard by the rest. "From the west."

"Spread out and cover down," Lattimer ordered. "Ain't *nobody* knows we're here. Wait for me to crack the first cap, then put at 'em!"

Fargo made a point of putting plenty of trees between himself and the gang. There was a good chance that whoever was approaching was criminal trash as low as Lattimer's gang—Pukes or Jayhawkers on the prowl. Even so, Fargo had no intention of cold-blooded murder. Every man he had been forced to kill, in his hard struggle to survive on the frontier, had been given an even chance.

Whoever was drawing near was taking few pains to move quietly. Only one rider, Fargo realized, moving slow. He heard the creak of saddle leather, and branches snapping as they were swiped from the rider's face.

Fargo had crouched behind a clump of hawthorn bushes, his Henry in his left hand, his Colt loosed but still holstered. He could just make out Dog Man on his left flank, sprawled behind a tree with his sawed-off double-twelve snapped into his shoulder.

A minute later a big seventeen-hand sorrel broke from the tree line, and Fargo's temples broke out in sweat.

The rider was an unequivocally fat man in a sheepskin coat with a six-pointed federal badge pinned to it—the U.S. marshal from Kansas City.

Fargo knew there was no time to think. He acted from pure reflex, spearing a flat stone that lay near his right foot and shipping it in hard at the sorrel's flank. The horse shied only a second before Lattimer opened up with his lever-action Volcanic rifle.

The slug punched into the lawman's canteen with a dull *thuck*. Fortunately for the marshal, his panicked horse couldn't decide whether to crow hop, sidestep, or rear, trying a little of all three at once. When Dog Man's scattergun roared, throwing out a deadly wall of blue whistlers, only a few of the pellets struck the horse.

Fargo pitched into the game, too, short iron leaping in his hand as he deliberately bucked his aim. To make it look good, however, he blew the marshal's hat spinning off his head as he finally made good his escape.

"Anybody tag the son of a bitch?" Lattimer demanded as the four men emerged from cover.

"I think he caught one of your slugs in his chest," Fargo lied. "I saw him clutch it when he rode out."

"Shit-fire!" Parsons exploded. "Something spooked his cockchafing horse. It's that lard-ass Evans from K.C. Fargo, your horse is rigged—that stallion of yours can outrun his own shadow. Ride the fat bastard down and finish him off."

"Nix on that, you hothead," Lattimer ordered. "He'll break for the open flats around the river. We kill that starman in plain view, there'll be a mob out here before you can say Jack Robinson. We'll have to move our camp now before he gets to town."

He turned to Fargo. "Get on back to Saint Joe and keep your ears open—we'll need to know how the wind sets. Read the newspapers, too, I ain't got no book learning. I'll let you know where to find us."

Fargo nodded and crossed toward the Ovaro. The bullet-savvy horse hadn't spooked during the gunfire. Fargo had just gripped the horn and stabbed a foot into the stirrup when Dog Man's voice arrested him.

"Fargo!"

The half-breed moved out of earshot of the other two. "I seen you throw that rock."

The sawed-off, with one lethal shell still chambered, was aimed center of mass on the Trailsman.

Fargo's armpits and groin suddenly oozed cold sweat when Dog Man clicked the hammer back. It was here, the Great Thing at last, and for some damn stupid reason Fargo regretted only that he hadn't had a woman the night before.

Suddenly Dog Man grinned and lowered his muzzle. "I seen it, Fargo, but I ain't sure whether you're a law dog yourself or just too woman-hearted to kill one."

"Neither one," Fargo ad-libbed. "Jude's tough as bore bristles, but he ain't the brightest spark in the campfire. I want that goddamn gold, and killing a U.S. marshal would trigger a manhunt that would drive all of us out of this area. It's easier to move your camp."

Dog Man mulled that while he tugged at his cauliflower ear. "You're slick, Fargo—slick as snot on a doorknob. That answer makes some sense—but not enough that I believe you."

Fargo said nothing, holding his face impassive.

"I'm enjoying this," Dog Man added. "Like you say—it adds savor. But pretty soon now I'm likely gonna have to kill you, and I ain't looking forward to it. You're a worthy bastard, for a fact you are."

"Dog Man!" Lattimer shouted. "Kiss your boyfriend good-bye and rustle up that cooking gear! We ain't got all mother-lovin' day!"

Dog Man grinned again, tossed Fargo a two-finger salute

and walked off. Fargo swung up onto the hurricane deck and wheeled the Ovaro, his heart still fear-hammering.

That was twice now, he warned himself, that he had underrated Dog Man. And he had a sinking feeling the third time would definitely not be the charm.

12

Fargo returned to town and managed to catch John Fowler at his hotel just as he was preparing to "work his traps" in the guise of a drummer plying his trade.

"Trouble," Fargo greeted him. "It looks like Lattimer's bunch is close to the next heist. They called me out to their camp today to sound me out on an escape plan."

Fowler, busy rigging his shoulder holster under his sack coat, frowned at this intelligence. "Christ, Pinkerton will fart blood. We can't let those three hyenas pull the job—we'll all become accessories if we don't report what we know before they strike. But once we put the kibosh on them, the principals will just cover their asses—maybe even disappear."

"You best take the word to Pinkerton," Fargo suggested. "I can't be sure who's watching me, and I'm pushing it with these daytime visits to his office. Also tell him they almost murdered a U.S. marshal today."

Fargo explained about Dave Evans's narrow escape and Lattimer's decision to move the camp.

"Brother, we better hit pay dirt *somewhere*," Fowler fretted. "Inge's sent word she's meeting Colonel Meriwether in a couple hours, something about lunch at her hotel. Maybe I'll have some luck when I search his house."

Fargo nodded. "I'll be watching Doyle. If he goes anywhere, I'll glom that shack of his."

"The door has a lock," Fowler said. "I already checked it out. You'll need your *passe-partout*."

"My who?"

"The bar-key Allan gave you. They're pretty handy—I'll be using mine on Meriwether's place. I used it a while back on Mayor Reece's house, too."

89

"Find anything?"

Fowler's moon face creased in a grin. "Just a wicked collection of whips in Lily's room. Tell me the straight—did she peel your hide?"

"That was her big idea, yeah. She got one lash in on me. Crazy little bitch."

"You going back for more?"

"She's on my mind," Fargo admitted. "But I'm steering clear—seems like every time a bird shits in this town, Lattimer and Parsons get a full report."

"Doyle," Fowler suggested.

"You know, I get the strong impression Lattimer knows and fears Doyle. But I'm not so sure he works for Lattimer. Matter fact, I don't see how he can be if he's trying to douse my glims. I'm convinced Lattimer's counting on me to get his ass to Mexico in one piece."

Fowler's eyes went distant. "Yeah, that's a poser, huh?"

Fargo watched his face closely. "You sure you're not hiding an ace? What's this hunch you mentioned?"

"Trailsman, on that score I got less than spider leavings. It's not a hunch like the one I had about Doyle—it's not a clue, not even an idea. It's what you might call an impression. You know how you sometimes close your eyes and a faint image lingers there for a second before it fades? That's all I got—mental vapors."

"You're protecting somebody," Fargo surmised as he headed for the door. "But I'm damned if I'll beat it out of you. Just remember—time is a bird, and the bird is on the wing."

Fargo returned to the livery and dug the detective kit Pinkerton had given him out of the straw where he'd hidden it. He removed the bar-key and headed out for the Adams Express office, secreting himself in an alley entrance across the street.

His vigil soon grew tiresome. He spotted Kirby Doyle several times, running food into the building and loading a freight wagon. Not until late afternoon did the man finally head on foot toward River Street and barrelhouse row.

This time, however, Fargo didn't follow him. He slipped quickly through the big wagon yard to the sloped-off shed behind the express office. Casting a quick glance around him in the brassy sunlight, Fargo examined the keyhole of a raw plank door.

Simple skeleton keys were sufficient to open most doors on the frontier, but the express office had opted for better security. The bar-key was actually a thin spindle with a slot into which fitted four separate, removable bits. Not until Fargo tried the third bit—fingers fumbling to remove the two ahead of it that didn't fit the lock—did the tumbler snap open.

Fargo's face wrinkled at the stench inside, hardly more bearable than the odor of a bat-board jakes. There was no window so he was forced to leave the door open until he lighted a stub of candle he found on an old nail keg.

One half of the large shed was chockablock with tools and parts, harness rigs, and tug chains. The other was Doyle's living area: A crude shakedown bunk, a three-legged stool and conical Sibley stove comprised the furnishings. Cross-stick shelves on one wall held some odds and ends such as a metal mirror, a leather strop and a straight razor, and a "yellow-back" book of the type filled with drawings of naked women.

The stench emanated from a brimming chamber pot and opened cans of food that had been partially eaten and were now growing nasty mold.

"The disgusting son of a bitch," Fargo muttered, being careful to breathe through his mouth only.

He was looking for a gun, but a cursory search turned up nothing. He began a more thorough search by peering under and behind the tools and parts.

His efforts turned up a big goose egg. Fargo next turned his attention to a disheveled heap of clothing and blankets at the foot of the shakedown. Again he found no weapons, but his knuckles brushed an old wool sock and he heard a metallic jangle.

Fargo turned the sock inside out and ten gold double eagles plopped out onto the shuck mattress.

Two hundred dollars—almost a year's pay for an enlisted soldier, more than a half-year's wages for a sheriff or cowboy. Way too damn much money, Fargo knew, for a shit-heel roustabout to have on hand.

True, it could represent careful savings over many years. But just last night Fargo had watched Doyle drink top-shelf whiskey and pay for the upstairs whores—how could a lowly mudsill burn up money like that and still manage to save any?

For a moment Fargo was tempted to pocket half the gold shiners—Septimus deserved another hundred dollars for that horse that was cut down. But Fargo's sense of fair play won out—despite being damn near convinced that Kirby Doyle was a paid killer, he couldn't yet prove it.

He had just dropped the shiners back into the sock when he heard a foot scrape outside. Fargo blew out the candle and leaped to one side of the door, cocking his right arm. In the half dimers, the storybook heroes were always bending a gun barrel over an enemy's head. Fargo, however, never turned a precision tool into a club except as a last resort.

A key clicked into the lock, then dead silence as whoever was outside realized the door was already unlocked. It meowed slowly open on rusted hinges and Doyle's long-haired head poked inside. Fargo's hard-hitting fist caught him in the sweet spot—along the jawline halfway between the ear and the point of his chin.

Doyle's head snapped to one side and he dropped as if he'd been poleaxed. Fargo quickly searched the unconscious man, discovering no weapons but twenty dollars in a hip pocket.

"Somebody's staking you, you dry-gulching bastard," Fargo muttered. "And you've got a piece hidden somewhere. When I catch you with it, we *will* be settling accounts."

His disappointment keen and his sense of urgency growing, Fargo stepped over Kirby Doyle and headed back to the livery.

"This has been an eventful day," Allan Pinkerton announced that evening at a hastily called meeting. "Fargo has learned that the next express holdup may be imminent. He's also discovered circumstantial evidence that Kirby Doyle *may* be in the mix somehow."

"What evidence?" Inge and Fowler chimed together.

"Money," Pinkerton said. "Too blasted much money in

the hands of a man who shouldn't even have two nickels to rub together. More than two hundred dollars, to be specific."

"With the spending habits of a prospector panning fat nuggets every day," Fargo added.

"That's certainly interesting," Inge conceded. "But what if he's just a garden-variety crook? Burke has mentioned to me that he thinks one of his employees is pilfering from the company."

"Yeah? Well, I had a little face-to-face with Doyle yesterday," Fargo said. "Coaxed him out a little, you might say. Lady, he's no chawbacon simpleton *or* a sneak thief. He's hard and mean and he's got the eyes of a stone-cold killer."

"Have you also read the bumps on his skull?" Inge teased. "This is a detective agency, Mr. Fargo. While I'm sure you and John really are shrewd judges of character, I agree with Allan—we operate on evidence, not hasty conclusions."

"Hear, hear," Pinkerton approved.

Fargo sent Inge a wry glance. "What are you—Doyle's Philadelphia lawyer?"

"I'm with Skye," Fowler put in, pacing in front of the big map of Missouri that covered half of one wall in Pinkerton's office. "Doyle wears the no-good label."

"Perhaps, but that may not be a point worth arguing at the moment," Pinkerton said. "John, tell them what you found today."

"While Sarah—I mean, Inge—had lunch with Colonel Meriwether, I searched his house. He's got quite a few papers and communiqués all tied to the gold shipments—official stuff you'd expect him to have given his job. But I went through the pockets of one of his tunics and I found a note that *doesn't* look so official. I copied it."

Pinkerton banged open the top drawer of his desk and pulled out a folded piece of paper, unfolding it and passing it to Inge first. She glanced at it, frowned, and handed it to Fargo. It took only a few seconds to read the thirteen-word message:

Send route soon as you can so we can figure out best approach.

                                                                        L.

"It's signed only 'L,' but it's certainly tempting," Pinkerton said, "to conclude it's from Lattimer."

Fargo's brow compressed with sudden puzzlement.

"Skye, why are you frowning?" Pinkerton demanded.

"Well, for one thing, it seems mighty damn stupid for a West Point man not to toss or burn a note like this—why would the colonel need to keep it like it was a love letter?"

Pinkerton sucked in his cheeks, mulling this point. "Perhaps he meant to and just forgot."

"You said 'for one thing,'" Fowler reminded the Trailsman. "What else bothers you?"

"Just today Lattimer told me to watch the newspapers—said he can't read. So how could he write this note?"

"That *is* puzzling," Pinkerton admitted.

"It's a pretty simple note," Fowler suggested. "And it was scrawled so I could barely read it. Half the words were misspelled—I cleaned it up when I copied it. Maybe Lattimer meant, Skye, that he can't read very good. You know how these inkslingers like to use thirty-five-cent words."

Inge said, "Yes, and besides all that—who's to say one of the other two didn't write it for him?"

Fargo nodded. "All that makes sense. Still, it seems a mite queer—the colonel keeping the note, I mean."

"In any event," Pinkerton said, "the letter 'L' hardly proves it's Lattimer. We have to pick cotton before we can make cloth. Inge, John, Skye—events are about to overtake us. We *must* exert ourselves, and quickly."

"Odd that you should mention cotton." Inge spoke up. "Meriwether is usually rather taciturn. But today he was more talkative. He spoke of a brother, one evidently very close to his heart, who made a cotton fortune in the rich black soil of east Texas. But two consecutive drought seasons have plunged him into debt—extreme debt. That might motivate a man to violate his military oath."

"Wouldn't be the first time," Fowler said.

"You kidding?" Fargo tossed in. "On the frontier, half the officers above the rank of captain are crooked as cat shit."

"More smokestacks and businessmen," Pinkerton said, "*that's* what this wild American West needs. Commerce has its thorns but will bring in effective law enforcement and quell these reckless elements."

"You mean well, Allan," Fargo said, "but you're full of sheep dip. You're just swapping for a better-dressed class of criminals. Manhattan is crawling with commerce and law-men, and yet street gangs control half the city after dark. And no offense to John here, but what makes these lawmen honest—a tin badge? There'll be criminals and crime so long as there's two men left on the earth."

"Which you should welcome, Allan, given your job," Fowler added.

Pinkerton actually brightened a little at this reminder. "So long as there's naught else for it, a man maun profit, eh? Still—some crimes have greater consequences than others. This case we're embarked on now . . ."

Pinkerton, like many immigrants, loved his adopted country passionately. He glanced at the American flag in a standard beside his desk, his face somber.

"This young nation is still an experiment. And unless a uniform monetary system can soon be put in place, I fear that experiment will fail. Just this morning I saw a man pay for his breakfast in Russian kopecks, and he was given change in Spanish *reals*! America remains a collection of competing regions following idiosyncratic rules and their own interests—look at this terrible situation unfolding in the Southern states and about to explode at any moment. A secure and consistent currency will help unify this country. And that cannot happen so long as road agents call the shots."

"We'll put the crusher on 'em," Fowler insisted.

"Yes," Pinkerton fretted, "but will we do it in time?"

During Pinkerton's heartfelt spiel Fargo had been study-ing his female partner. Her hair was down this evening, tum-bling in a pale blond confusion to the middle of her back. The room was warm and she had slipped her lace shawl off, baring creamy white, finely sculpted shoulders and—thanks to the low décolleté of her red velvet gown—a tantalizing view of her cleavage.

"Is there a fly on my nose, Mr. Fargo?" she asked him curtly. "Or haven't you lifted your eyes that high yet?"

"I don't get it," he said. "Your sex is what you trade in—you've got three horny men trailing you, and they don't care a jackstraw about your 'breeding.' So why come the haughty lady with me just for enjoying a harmless peek?"

She took a deep breath, expelled a fluming sigh. "Mr. Fargo—Skye—I've enjoyed sparring with you, but now I feel it's time to clear the air. Evidently you are confusing appearances with reality. I was not born to wealth, I am not now wealthy, and I have never *been* wealthy. Nor am I, as you imply, a social elitist. I am a product of what is euphemistically known as genteel poverty, which really means that I am well educated but haven't a dollar to show for it."

"Sarah," Pinkerton interrupted awkwardly, "you don't need to—"

She raised a peremptory hand, still watching Fargo. "My father taught Latin at a boys' school in Fort Wayne, Indiana. He died when I was sixteen. I now support an ailing mother and two younger siblings."

She drew her shawl around her finely sculpted shoulders and stood up, those piercing eyes like two brilliant blue gems fixed on Fargo.

"I have turned down several offers of marriage because—somewhat like yourself—I am of an independent and contrary nature. Not once have I compromised my virtue in pursuit of a living, and based on what I've heard of *your* amorous pursuits, you have no right whatsoever to look down your nose at me."

"Amorous pursuits?" Fargo repeated, his lips twitching in a grin.

She ignored him. "For the sake of this difficult case, I hope we can cooperate fully—especially as I rather like you and suspect that, beneath your rough and cynical exterior, you are a man of honor. Shabby honor, perhaps, but honor nonetheless."

With that she flounced out in a froufrou of whispering skirts. Fowler dashed out after her.

Pinkerton aimed a withering glance at Fargo. "Anything to add to that?"

"Yeah. She's a good actress."

"That was not acting, you dunderhead!"

Fargo heaved out of the chair and clapped on his hat. "Don't be a simp. She's delivered that pretty little speech plenty of times. Anyway, she just wasted her breath. I like her, too. Like her just fine."

"God help me," Pinkerton lamented. "I was afraid this would happen."

13

Fargo caught up with Fowler and Inge before they had walked a half block.

"You can let go of that short iron, John," Fargo said when Fowler spun around. "I'm a friendly cuss. Mind if I walk with you two?"

"Actually," Fowler replied, "as much as I enjoy Sar—I mean, Inge's company, would you mind walking her to the Patee? I need to visit a gambling house on Center Street where the mayor likes to throw money down a rat hole."

He tipped his stiff felt bowler at Inge and left abruptly before Fargo could comment.

"I hope he doesn't think I was crowding him out," Fargo said as he fell in step with the pretty operative.

"More likely he knows your reputation with the fair sex and didn't want to be in the way as the 'master' sets to work."

"That's a libel on me," Fargo protested, but so insincerely that they both laughed.

"Allan thinks very highly of John Fowler," she went on. "And I've learned he's a courageous man."

"He is that in spades," Fargo agreed. "But courage isn't nerve. Courage will get a man into a fight, but only nerve will win it for him. Fowler's got nerve—plenty and to spare."

"You seem to know whereof you speak."

"I suspect you know something about nerve, too. Pinkerton may love to speechify but he's a good judge of character."

"Does that bother you—a woman having nerve, I mean?"

"In a horse *or* a woman it's a good thing."

She laughed, a musical lilt that Fargo suspected had claimed many male hearts. "You do have a pithy way about you. I suspect you're quite direct in everything you do."

"And I suspect you're not," Fargo countered.

He felt her eyes on him in the dim streetlight although her face was mostly in shadow. "Well, *that* was too direct to call an innuendo. You don't think I'm honest?"

"I never said that," Fargo assured her, "although I doubt you're sainted. A woman who can juggle three powerful men can't be *too* honest. It's a kind of acting, and I'm told the best actors can't help becoming what they pretend to be."

This time she stopped walking, looking at him even more intently. She stood close enough that Fargo could smell the honeysuckle scent of her perfume, the clean tang of her hair. And the more subtle, alluring odor of femininity that made his manhood suddenly, insistently hard.

"Yes," she finally said as if thinking aloud, "you wear buckskins with traces of old blood on them and carry a vicious-looking knife in your boot. But now I see that your mind is hardly rustic. This is a side of you the penny press ignores."

"What would you expect for a penny?" he riposted and again they both laughed.

"Finally, a hearty laugh," she said as they resumed walking. "You act as if it's taking medicine just to smile at me."

They engaged in mostly inconsequential banter until they reached the long green awning in front of the Patee.

"You know," she told him, her voice husky and low now, "as a supposed rich woman of the world there's no problem with having male visitors in my room."

"Even one wearing bloody buckskins and a vicious knife?"

"Like all discreet hotels catering to the wealthy, the Patee has a private entrance that bypasses the lobby."

"Then I say let's bypass it."

She led him around to a carved-oak door and unlocked it, tugging Fargo up several flights of stairs to the top floor. The suite of rooms she occupied was fit for a visiting rajah: a sitting room appointed with Persian rugs and teakwood furniture, with varnished oil paintings in gold scrollwork frames and a velvet pull-rope for summoning maids and porters.

"Since you're so direct," she said in a low, throaty voice, "I shall be also. The bedroom is this way."

She took his hand and led him through a dressing room with a gilt-edged triple-vanity mirror to an opulent bedroom with a huge canopied bed at its center.

Fargo had laid his guns aside in some fancy rooms, but this one was the topper—and the woman now shimmying out of her dress was as near to perfection as any in Fargo's memory. Her unrestrained tangle of blond hair glowed like spun gold in the flattering lamplight as she pulled an embroidered chemise over her head, then stepped out of her frilly pantaloons.

She stood before him naked, her full, heart-shaped lips moist and glistening. Fargo felt the sex need in him, hot blood pounding in his temples and making his rigid man gland diamond hard. His eyes raked over her from the Greek-goddess face to the strawberry-tipped, firm breasts, and lower to the silky mons bush only one shade darker than her hair. Her legs, like the rest of her, were perfectly shaped and proportioned from the creamy ivory thighs and supple calves to the well-turned ankles.

"I'm not as wild and violent as Lily Reece," she said in a voice just above a whisper. "But why don't you strip and see if quiet girls can be passionate lovers?"

"I like quiet girls," Fargo assured her truthfully. "Noise just distracts me."

She stared in fascination, as he peeled his shirt off, at the hard, sloping pectorals and corded muscles on his arms and shoulders. Nor could she miss the old scars left by bullets, knives and arrow points.

But when Fargo kicked out of his boots and shucked his trousers, her awe was complete.

"My stars and garters," she said breathlessly, staring mesmerized at the impressive curved saber leaping with his heartbeat. "It's not just your reputation that's big."

Fargo tasted those moist lips, their tongues hungrily exploring, then swept her up, thrilling at the satin feel of her skin. He dropped her onto the bed and placed a palm on each inner thigh, parting her legs wide. The heady musk of her ready sex wafted to his nostrils, egging him on.

She shuddered hard beneath him, grinding her tits against the matted hair of his chest, when he probed her honeyed portal open with the tip of his staff and then bucked his hips, plunging in deep and taking her hard and fast as his lust demanded. She met each stroke and urged him on by cupping her hands on his ass and pulling him into her, fuel on fuel to the fire raging in his loins.

She was indeed a quiet lover, crying out sharply only when a powerful chain of climaxes washed over her; she wrapped her legs tightly around Fargo and milked him hard with the tight velvet grip of her love muscle until he, too, shuddered hard as he exploded inside her, needing a half-dozen strong, conclusive thrusts to spend himself.

Both of them lost all track of time, or even awareness, so depleted were they from the force of their erotic passion. But Skye Fargo, who had satisfied the wanting of more women than he could possibly remember, knew that this one had forever notched a spot in his gallery of memorable lovers.

Shortly after his pleasant interlude with Inge, Fargo finally got his chance to meet Mayor Josiah Reece—but the circumstances were hardly cordial.

He knew, the moment he swung open the big front doors of the livery barn, that he was up against it. Septimus Perkins, his face grim and pale, stood with two other men about halfway inside the barn—in front of the stall Fargo had been sleeping in.

One of the two men with him wore a star on his rawhide vest and had a homely face flat as a skillet. The other, better dressed and slightly older, was portly and bespectacled. He stared at something in the stall, something that made his face look like he had been drained by leeches.

The star-packer held a .31 Colt aimed at Fargo. "Toss down that lead-chucker, Trailsman."

Fargo ignored him, looking a question at Septimus.

"Fargo," the old hostler said, his voice tight from emotion, "this is Sheriff Harney Winslowe and Mayor Reece."

Fargo nodded. "All right, Sheriff, what's the charge?"

"As if you didn't know, you woman-killing son of a bitch!" Reece spat out.

Alarm tightened Fargo's nape. He took a few more paces toward them, halting when Winslowe thumb-cocked the

Colt. The sound seemed loud and menacing in the stillness of the barn.

"I don't chew my cabbage twice, Fargo," the lawman warned. "Reach that six-shooter out *slow* with just your thumb and pointing finger and then drop it."

Fargo did as ordered and then covered the rest of the distance to the stall, peering in. The gruesome—yet oddly compelling—sight made his heart sit out the next few beats.

Lily Reece lay dead in the straw, her neck twisted at an impossible angle. She had died with abject terror starched deep into her pretty features. Her copper-tinted hair was fanned out in a mane, putting Fargo in mind of the farthingaled Madonna he'd seen on religious tracts.

"*Shoot* the murdering bastard, Harney!" Reece urged. "Look what he did to my girl! I'll say he tried to run."

"Yeah, but I won't," Septimus spoke up.

"I'm not hell-bent on peddling lead, Mayor," Winslowe said. "We ain't heard Fargo's side of it."

Some sights, Fargo realized, still staring at the murdered woman, got stuck on a man's eyelids. This was one he would carry to the grave. He averted his eyes and looked another question at Septimus.

"I never seen anything to equal it, Skye," the liveryman said in a flat, toneless voice. "I got cozy with the jug right after supper and passed out drunk as the lords of Creation by nine o'clock or thereabouts. Your Ovaro woke me up mebbe an hour later, prac'ly kicking down his stall. I went back to see what all the commotion was and . . . and found her."

Mayor Reece wore a long gray duster to protect his suit. "If I was heeled, Fargo, you'd be sucking wind by now, you low-crawling, woman-killing—"

"Sheathe your horns, Mayor," Winslowe advised. "Fargo, can you account for your actions in the past couple hours?"

"My dead girl proves his actions," Reece sputtered. "The son of a bitch raped her, then killed her to shut her mouth about it."

"I take exception to that," Fargo said mildly. To him Reece was just another pasty-faced barber's clerk, a member of that group Fargo dismissed as soft-handed bastards who lived in towns. And he might damn well be a criminal, too.

But the man had just lost a daughter to violent murder, and Fargo couldn't imagine much that would be harder to bear.

"You *take exception*? Don't think your got-up reputation will save you—you don't stand deuce-high against me, not in *this* town."

"Where you been the last couple hours?" Sheriff Winslowe repeated. "She's fresh killed."

"With a woman," Fargo replied, leaving it there.

"Oh, he's been with a woman, all right," Reece snarled, "and there she lies."

"Mayor, sell your ass," Septimus put in. "Why in tarnal hell would Fargo kill your girl and just *leave* her here while he went off—leave her here where he's staying so's I could find her? It don't make no sense. Some filthy cockroach left her here to frame him."

Reece was too agitated to credit this remark, but Winslowe seemed to be mulling it.

"Mayor," Winslowe said, "my inclination would be to arrest Jack Parsons—he was the one dogging her all the time, and you know how she led him on. But I got no idea where the hell he stays."

"Parsons," Reece repeated almost to himself as if remembering something. "Lily told me it was drunks that shot up my house the other night. But I found out the truth. Fargo and Parsons shot it out over Lily. Maybe . . . just maybe . . ."

By now Fargo was convinced who the killer was—the man who had been shadowing him almost since his arrival in town; the man who had fired into the Reece parlor when Parsons was out at his camp; the man who had fired at Fargo a second time, killing a horse instead; the man who Fargo had knocked senseless earlier today, and the man who had now decided it might be easier to frame Skye Fargo than to kill him.

"It's always possible it was Jack Parsons," Fargo said, "but I don't think so."

"Why not?" Winslowe demanded. "I don't know a damn thing about the man 'cept he done prison time."

"He has, and I'd lay odds he's murdered others. But I don't like him for this crime."

"Hell's bells, Trailsman! He's perfect for it. It's all over town how you dusted his doublet right out in the street and then fuc—"

Winslowe caught himself in the nick of time, glancing at Reece. "I mean, and then went to visit Lily. Who's to say he didn't do this to frame you and get revenge on *both* of you?"

"Hell, Sheriff, why should I argue against a theory that takes the cootie off of me? But I don't think it was Parsons—I suggest you talk to Kirby Doyle."

"Doyle?" the sheriff repeated incredulously. "You been nibbling peyote? Sure, he's a no-'count bummer, but *he* ain't no murderer."

Fargo realized his mistake and dropped the subject of Doyle. He'd already encountered this reaction from Pinkerton and Inge, even Lattimer's gang.

Winslowe, however, seemed to bethink himself. "Say . . . Septimus just told me somebody recently tried to put you with your ancestors. Any connection to this—or Doyle?"

By now Fargo realized he would have to settle this account himself. In his way Fargo felt sorry for the well-intended sheriff. Frontier lawmen spent most of their time collecting taxes, jugging drunks, running meals to prisoners and catching dogs. Solving this heinous crime was beyond his competency.

"If there is any connection," he lied, "it's too far north for me to figure out."

Josiah Reece spoke up impatiently. "Sheriff, I'm the mayor of this city and I'm ordering you to arrest Fargo. Granted, there's at least one other suspect in Jack Parsons. But Fargo has no alibi except a woman he refuses to name."

"I don't believe I'm going to let myself be arrested, Mayor," Fargo said quietly. "You got no link between me and that poor girl's body. No witness saw me with her today. You ain't even got a motive—'rape,' my hairy white ass. If you truly want the killer brought to justice, jugging me won't help anything."

"Damn you to hell, Fargo, *I'm* the—"

"Now look, Josiah," Winslowe cut him off. "I'm damned if I'll stand here over a murdered woman and paint her name black. *No* woman deserves this. But you know damn good and well your daughter was . . . well, she had a wild, dangerous streak in her. She played fast and loose with plenty of men who ain't exactly known for walking the straight and narrow."

The mayor's stone-eyed silence confirmed this.

The sheriff added, "I ain't never heard of no serious shadow on Fargo's name—a few scandals involving females, sure, and it's got him some buckshot in his hind end. And he's been charged for violating Sunday blue laws and piddling shit like that. But he'd no sooner lift a hand to hurt a woman than you or me."

Reece cast another glance at his only child, now lying dead and growing cold, and seemed on the verge of losing control of his feelings.

"Ahh, Christ . . . you're right, Harney. This wouldn't be Fargo's style at all. Somebody's trying to railroad him to the gallows."

He looked at Fargo, pushing his spectacles higher on the bridge of his nose. "I'm sorry I lost my temper, Fargo. It's just—it's—"

Sudden tears spilled from his eyes and Fargo stepped closer to put a steadying hand on his shoulder. In that moment he didn't care if Reece *was* part of the syndicate— he spoke to the father's grief.

"No, Mayor, I'm the one who's sorry— sorry this had to happen to Lily and to you. And I give you my word, it won't stand."

"Leave this to the law," Winslowe said gruffly, finally leathering his shooter.

"Law is power," Fargo said, "not justice. If you can solve this, fine. Any man who murders a woman won't live to dance on air. But if law comes a cropper, I won't."

"Fargo, it bears reminding you—this is an organized state, not a territory. There's a duty to retreat if you can avoid violence, and settling scores on your own is vigilantism—a felony in Missouri."

"That's too rich for my belly, Sheriff. This whole damn state is lousy with murdering cutthroats that kill a man for his boots. Retreat? Retreat to where? Too often it's kill or be killed, and you know it. Sometimes the only way to survive in Misery is to make a clean jerk every time."

"Amen," Septimus said, taking a last look at Lily Reece and turning away.

"I ain't asking you to crawfish, Fargo," Winslowe said, not unkindly. "Just to respect the law."

"I respect it," Fargo said, "insofar as I can."

Winslowe nodded and forced out a long sigh. "All right, Josiah. Let's go find the undertaker."

14

Fargo rode out the next morning before the dew had dried, his thoughts rough and ugly—especially when they turned to Kirby Doyle, woman killer.

A messenger had come to the livery last night reciting a terse message from Lattimer: *Two miles west of the last camp, fire a shot. Wait and we'll guide you in.*

It had required all of Fargo's considerable self-control, last night after the undertaker hauled off Lily Reece's body, not to hunt down Doyle and kill him on the spot. But too many nagging reasons stayed his hand.

For starters, despite his deep convictions, he still had no real proof Doyle was in fact the killer—indeed, that he was even a serious criminal. The gold double eagles in that sock proved nothing. Yes, Fargo's confrontation with Doyle in the wagon yard left the Trailsman convinced—deep in his blood consciousness—that Doyle was a dangerous killer. But belief alone was no justification for killing a man.

Besides, killing him now in the heat of emotion might bollix up Pinkerton's crucial case. Fargo was damn near certain that Doyle was working for someone connected to the express robberies, but a person who was keeping Doyle's role separate from Lattimer and his gang. If so, killing him too soon could ruin key evidence.

Thus ruminating, his thoughts dangerously distracted, Fargo reacted too late to a clear warning sign. He was riding the grassy bank of the Missouri, bearing south from Saint Joe, when a flock of jays just ahead of him suddenly took flight. The few seconds it took Fargo to shift his thoughts fully back to the here and now proved to be his undoing.

A group of five riders suddenly emerged from the thick

brush just ahead of him. Fargo heard more cut him off from behind. The moment he recognized their butternut-dyed homespun, he tasted coppery fear.

Pukes. He had ridden smack into the trap of some of the most vicious killers in America.

The Ovaro halted without having to be reined in, snorting nervously. Fargo stared into the muzzles of a motley but deadly collection of firearms, ranging from Springfield breech-loaders to a daunting pepperbox pistol with six barrels that fired at once.

"Well now, mister, looks like you got your tit in a wringer, hanh?"

The speaker and apparent ringleader was a filthy, wall-eyed ruffian astride a sore-used piebald. He wore a greasy flop hat with burn marks from being used as a potholder. He kneed his horse closer and Fargo saw beggar's-lice on the Puke's clothing.

Fargo cast a quick glance at the men siding him. Some of these hard-eyed drifters may have started out as mere range bums, but they were all easy-go killers now. It was a plentiful commodity produced in the bloody cauldron of Missouri politics and race hatred.

"That's one fine-looking horse," walleye said. "Yessiree. Oughter fetch at least five hunnert dollars, hey?"

"Thereabouts," Fargo agreed in a voice much calmer than he felt.

"Now, boys," the leader said, flashing a grin full of yellow and crooked teeth, "this tall hombre don't size up like no good ol' boy. What we got here, chappies, is a maverick. And y'all know the law of the range: Any maverick is for the taking. And so is anything they own."

"I got dibs on that Henry rifle," spoke up a rodent-faced man on a swayback mule.

Despite the morning chill Fargo felt sweat oozing out from under his hatband. But long discipline made him fight down his fear and put it outside of himself. *The readiness was all . . .*

"You're a quiet motherfucker, ain't ya?" walleye goaded him. "Usually they start begging by now. You pissed yourself yet?"

Several of the men laughed.

Walleye grinned at his own wit. Then he said, "Well, I ain't one to mealymouth, mister. You done seen your last sunrise."

"This no-dick son of a bitch looks like a Jayhawker abolitionist to me, Weed," rat face taunted.

It was only seconds away, Fargo realized. A piece of lice-infested garbage would twitch his trigger finger and cancel out Fargo's life as casually as swatting a fly—cancel his history, his memories, all the vitality within him that was still his due on earth. Only seconds away, and Fargo would have one chance: something the Mexicans called the *paso de la muerte*, "the stunt of death." It came down to this place and this time, and if he made one slight mistake, waited a heartbeat too long, there was only eternal darkness, eternal oblivion.

The readiness was all . . .

"That right, mister?" walleye goaded Fargo. "You believe burr heads got souls like John Brown preaches?"

"You got a soul?" Fargo responded quietly.

"I'm a white man, ain't I? All white men got souls."

"Good," Fargo said. "That means you believe in hell, too. And from now to eternity it's hot pitchforks for you."

Quicker than thought Fargo filled his hand and an eye-blink later a neat hole appeared in walleye's forehead. Fargo, his lips a grim, determined slit, pressured the Ovaro with his knees in an urgent way the stallion recognized.

The Ovaro hunkered on his hocks, leaped almost straight up, twisted 180 degrees in midair, and hit the ground running in the opposite direction. The maneuver was so impressive that most of the Pukes sat slack-jawed for a few moments in utter disbelief.

Three men formed the rearguard. Fargo fired three times in three seconds, killing two of them and blowing the jaw off the third. With no letup he twisted sideways in the saddle and dropped two of the horses in the forward group. This left only two riders to pursue him, but in the corner of his eye Fargo saw more Pukes boiling out from the thickets.

The all-important element of surprise bought him only a few seconds. Fargo lit out like a scalded dog, knowing he was dead if he didn't get out of the weather pronto.

It was his carefully made mind maps that convinced

Fargo to turn north. The Ovaro's superior speed and stamina were of little use in this thickly grown, heavily wooded area, especially with the wide Missouri cutting off any escape to the west. But Fargo remembered a narrow defile about three hundred yards ahead, a narrow, traversable opening that led to a steep hogback ridge. If he could gain the high ground, he and his 16-shot Henry could hold off a regiment.

His Colt was empty so Fargo bent lower over the Ovaro's neck and urged him to reckless speed. Rifles and short irons crackled behind him, rounds snapping past his ears. A thunder of hooves told him a good-size force was in pursuit.

The Ovaro was eating up the landscape so rapidly that Fargo almost missed the entrance to the defile. He tugged rein hard right, and his stalwart stallion, dangerously skidding, plunged into the narrow incline.

The hogback, a ridge with a sharp crest and abruptly sloping sides, loomed out ahead. Halfway up, the Ovaro was lathered and heaving from the hard pace and steep climb. But with bullets whiffing all around them, some so close Fargo felt the wind rip, they gained the crest.

Safe on the backside, Fargo leaped to the ground and tugged his Henry from its sheath. He returned to the crest, dropped into a kneeling-offhand position, and racked a bullet into the chamber. Twice the Henry kicked into his shoulder, wiping the two lead Pukes from their saddles. That broke the back of the attack, and Fargo chased the rest off with a half dozen more shots.

Only now, with his enemy vanquished, did Fargo let the fact of almost certain death sink in. His arms were suddenly so weak that he had to ground the Henry as strength deserted his limbs for a full minute.

Just before he heaved himself to his feet, however, he caught sight of the Ovaro. Fargo fell back to the ground in paroxysms of laughter.

The stallion was calmly taking off the scant grass, tail lazily shooing away flies as if he'd merely been put out to pasture.

"Well, old warhorse," Fargo called down to him. "I reckon Pukes don't stand so high in your estimation?"

By way of pithy response, the Ovaro lifted his tail and dropped several fresh horse apples onto the side of the ridge.

Despite Lattimer's instructions, Fargo didn't risk sending a gunshot signal so the gang could guide him in to their new camp. Instead, the veteran tracker followed the clear sign beginning at the old spot near the river.

"Fargo riding in!" he called out.

It was a good spot. Only one approach in the thick trees, with a sand-bottom creek running through it.

"Christ, you're still above the ground?" Dog Man greeted him. "Sounded like a war back near the river."

"How the hell did you find us?" Parsons demanded.

"He's a tracker, you knucklehead," Lattimer replied. "Who jumped you, Fargo? Law dogs?"

"Pukes." Fargo swung down and led the Ovaro to the creek, throwing the bridle and letting him tank up. Today, Fargo noticed, Dog Man had whipped up a veritable feast of sowbelly and corn dodgers. Fargo pulled a corn dodger from the ashes, Parsons scowling.

Lattimer sat with his back to a pine tree, shoveling his food in. "Any word on that fat-ass marshal you think I plugged?"

Fargo shook his head. "Too soon to be in the newspapers. I wouldn't worry about it, though—Saint Joe has a bigger story."

"Well, you got a fish bone caught in your throat? Spit it out."

"The mayor's daughter was murdered last night."

Fargo watched Parsons carefully as he said this. The man's astounded reaction instantly convinced Fargo that Jack Parsons had nothing to do with the killing—not that he had ever suspected him. His fork stopped halfway to his mouth, and his face turned white as new gypsum.

"The crazy redhead?" Lattimer said between bites, obviously unperturbed. "Who done for her?"

"Nobody knows," Fargo replied. "But the killer tried to blame me for it."

Fargo briefly explained his tense reception in the livery last night. When he finished Dog Man chuckled.

"Looks like that wild little whore finally got her come-uppance," he said. "She liked it rough and *rough* is what she got."

"Good timing, too," Lattimer said. "Fargo's right. With the whole town wondering who killed that whore, ain't too likely they'll much give a big one about Dave Evans gettin' ambushed."

"Sure," Dog Man said. "And with Pukes in the area, won't be nothing to fret about if that badge-toter bled out some-wheres. Yeah boy, that little whore done us all a favor by gettin' herself killed."

"*Both* you yahoos sew up your lips!" Parsons blurted out, tossing his food aside and heaving to his feet. He began pacing in a circle like a caged lion, clenching and unclenching his fists. He looked at Fargo.

"Who do you think done it?"

"Sheriff Winslowe seems to like you for it. But he doesn't know where to find you. Personally, I think it was Kirby Doyle."

"Killing a *woman*!" Parsons spat out.

"What of it?" Lattimer said. "I gutted a whore in Santa Fe for picking my pockets."

Parsons didn't seem to hear him. "Hell, so what if she was a little wild? The spineless, filthy . . . I'm gonna kill whoever done it."

"You ain't gonna do shit about it," Lattimer admonished. "That whip-crackin' bitch ain't our lookout. So just get over your peeve."

Dog Man slanted a sly, conspiratorial glance at Fargo. "Plenty of men talk the he-bear talk, Jack. But when it comes time to burn powder their knees play them false."

"A *woman*!" Parsons repeated, not even registering Dog Man's taunt. "A gal what just liked to have fun. Why, she—"

"Whack the cork," Lattimer snapped. "Nerve up, you fool, and bottle all this revenge talk. We got a big job comin' on. A man who worries about fleas will get et by tigers. Flush that dead whore outta your headpiece."

Lattimer looked at Fargo again, pulling several gold coins from his pocket. "Any day now, Fargo, we all got to be ready to hit leather. Take this and get them horseshoes made.

Stock us up good on grub and tobacco, too, and some liquor. There's gonna be some killing before we get that bullion, and if we don't light out fast afterwards we're gonna be in one world of shit."

Fargo returned to Saint Joseph, fighting shy of the area where he'd been waylaid by border ruffians, and turned the Ovaro over to Septimus. Then he hoofed it to River Street and woke John Fowler up at his hotel.

"I was up till late running my traps," he explained when he let Fargo in. "All I got for it was air pudding. I—"

He suddenly noticed that Fargo's face was powder-blackened. "Jehoshaphat! Looks like you had one hell of a cartridge session."

"I thought I was gone beaver," Fargo admitted. "Rode right into a trap. Some Pukes took a shine to my stallion."

"And you added some lead to their diet."

Fargo grinned, watching the former constable wiggle into his shoulder rig. "Oh, we had an enlightening discussion about the human soul first."

Fargo eased himself carefully into the rickety chair. "Then I rode out to palaver with Lattimer. We got damn little time, John. Lattimer ordered me to stock up on horseshoes and eats."

Fowler scrubbed his face with his hands, trying to wake up. "Yeah, we got to pop this pimple and pop it quick."

"There's another burr under our saddle," Fargo said. "That damn cunning half-breed Dog Man. He suspects me. He's having fun playing the larks with me, but he's unstable nitro. He's also smart as a steel trap and he doesn't miss a trick. He could cold deck me at any time."

Fowler nodded glumly. "It's coming down to the nut cutting, all right, and we need a break. The best evidence we got is that note I found in Meriwether's tunic, and I was too stupid to take it. Might be, we coulda matched it up to the writing of somebody in the gang."

"I'll tell you flat out—I doubt if any of those three owlhoots can read or write."

Fowler's eyebrows tented in confusion. "I don't catch your drift. You think somebody besides the gang wrote it?"

"Somebody," Fargo said cryptically. "Anyhow, you had no warrant to search the colonel's house, remember? Even if they did write it, it could never be used in court like Pinkerton keeps harping. It still bothers me that Meriwether didn't destroy that note. Criminals are stupid, but not his caliber of criminal—if he is one."

Fowler nodded. "Yeah, that rings right. Besides, we can't put the needle just on Meriwether. Inge saw Reece pass something to him at the Hathaway House."

"She did say that," Fargo said quietly, watching Fowler closely. But the former lawman was working things out aloud and paid scant attention to the remark.

"Reece," Fowler repeated. "It was all over town about Lily and how you almost got jugged for killing her. But the thing of it is—Reece lives in that big house with the fancy gingerbread work under the eaves. Persian rugs and fancy furniture freighted in . . . how can he afford a lay like that on a mayor's salary?"

"He can't, but he ain't the first weasel-dick politician to live beyond his means."

"No, but I happen to know he's poor shakes at the gambling tables, so that can't explain it. Night before last, I watched him drop over a hundred dollars in two hours. Bought drinks for the house, too. And Inge says he's a big spender."

"Inge's a damn smart woman," Fargo said. "And damn beguiling too. Seems like she spends most of her time with Hardiman Burke. But she hasn't got much to report about him, has she?"

Fowler's eyes ran from his. "No, I guess not."

"No. I've noticed something else a mite queer. She bends over backwards to throw any suspicion off Kirby Doyle, yet she won't do the same for Colonel Meriwether."

This time Fowler did meet Fargo's gaze. "Go ahead, Trailsman. I'm listening."

"Doyle has done a damn good job of convincing people all his biscuits aren't done. Nobody pays a never-mind to a soft brain. But me and you know better. We also know that the syndicate—whoever that is—gave the go-ahead to Lattimer to hire me. And since Doyle tried to kill me, then frame me for killing Lily Reece, he's sure's hell not working for the syndicate—not all the time, anyhow."

"Yeah, and Reece wouldn't order his own daughter killed, so *he's* not paying Doyle."

"The way you say," Fargo agreed. "So who the hell *is* paying him?"

Fowler, face concentrating hard, answered slowly and carefully. "If Burke is topkick for the operation, it can't be him. That leaves only Meriwether unless there's somebody we don't know about yet."

Fargo's relentless, penetrating blue eyes bored into him. "You sure about that?"

Fowler sat down on the bed, his eyes glazing over.

"Maybe it's high time to tell me about this hunch of yours," Fargo coaxed. "It's about Inge, right?"

Fowler nodded once, his face a mask of misery. "That's why I butted out so quick last night. I wanted you to get a better impression of the woman. I trust your instincts. And unlike me and most other men, you're no sap when it comes to beautiful women."

"You fell for her, huh?"

"Head over heels the first time I met her. What *is* your impression of her?"

"A woman that beautiful and smart, all the men in town in love with her . . . well, she's damn dangerous *if* she has the moral rot. Something about her doesn't tally, but I can't say what. But you know something I don't and it's time to spill it."

"Maybe I do, but I ain't sure. It was about two, three days before you arrived in Saint Joe. See, sometimes Inge would signal to me from her hotel room using her dark lantern. You know, to tell me if it was clear to meet with her. With her stringing three men along, I couldn't be sure when one of them might be with her in her room."

Fowler paused, working his hands into fists. "Well, on this one night, I happened to be following Hardiman Burke. We were getting close to the Patee when a street melee broke out, maybe a dozen teamsters brawling. I got knocked down and by the time I fought my way free, I'd lost Burke."

Fowler, clearly agitated, stood up and began pacing the small room.

"I went straight to the hotel but saw no sign of him. I just happened to glance up to Inge's window and I saw her signaling to somebody with her dark lantern. Christ, I like to died when I saw that. Allan was out of town that day, so it wasn't him."

Fargo said, "Was she expecting you to be down there?"

"Now see, right there is why I kept my mouth shut all this time. I *was* supposed to be coming by, but not until a half hour later. There could've been a mix-up on the time, or—or she could've been signaling to Reece, Meriwether or anybody else."

"Like maybe Kirby Doyle?" Fargo suggested quietly.

Fowler halted and his jaw slacked open. "You don't think . . . I mean—"

Fargo raised a hand to cut him off. "No, I *don't* think so. I'm just puzzling it out. Burke, Reece and Meriwether are well-dressed toffs—you already said they were in the habit of visiting her room."

"Yeah, I take your drift. Why would she have to send signals to any of them when they could just go up? But Doyle—sure, there's a private entrance and all, but *if* he was her secret dirt worker, she wouldn't run that chance."

Fargo nodded. "That's how I see it, too."

"I been in a sweat over this, Skye. It's got me plumb bumfuzzled. I wanted to talk to Pinkerton about it, but that would have been telling him she was maybe sandbagging his entire operation."

"Yeah, and the prideful peacock would've cashiered you on the spot for even hinting it. He considers his character judgment whatchacallit—infallible. And family man or no, just like you he's struck a spark for that blond beauty."

Fowler sat heavily on the bed, slowly shaking his head as if after a hard punch. "She can't be running the show—Allan didn't bring her out here until after the first two heists. But I just can't believe her and the syndicate are feeding at the same trough."

"There's no reason to *believe* it—all we got so far is riverwater soup. But *if* she's in this deal somehow, it doesn't seem likely Meriwether is her pard—not the way she's talking against him."

"Which means she—or maybe Doyle using her barkey—mighta planted that note in the colonel's tunic. And don't forget, she claimed to see Reece pass something to the colonel. Like you said—Burke is the only one she's reported nothing on."

Fargo forced out a long, nasal sigh, turning his gaze toward the flyspecked window. A cloudless sky, blue as a gas flame, made him wish he was shut of this town, of *all* towns. Only a few blocks away he could see the night train from Hannibal easing to a stop under the water tower, boilers venting huge, billowing white clouds of steam.

Progress. So far none of the railroads had built tracks west of the Missouri, but soon the contracts would be inked, the backroom deals made, and "railroad law" would tyrannize even the far frontier. Tammany politics, robber barons, more criminal syndicates like the one he was now fighting—all of it was coming trailing hell in its wake.

Fowler's voice, a study in misery, startled him back to the present. "You think she's guilty, Skye?"

"I think both of us could be full of shit up to our eyeballs. All we really got is some lantern signals that could've been an honest mix-up. The rest of it is a bunch of 'ifs' and 'ands.' But here's what I don't like—her being guilty explains things that her being innocent doesn't."

"Yeah. Well, I'll tell you this much—we don't dare go to Pinkerton without real proof. We have to work this trail out ourselves."

Fargo unfolded from the chair, "And I'll tell *you* something. We're down to bedrock and showing damn little color. There's three killers expecting me to join them any time now for the biggest heist of all. We got to move full bore, Constable, and hope like hell we can pull a rabbit or two out of a hat."

15

The moment Fargo rounded the front corner of the Ozark Hotel he spotted Kirby Doyle.

The man stood on the opposite side of River Street, obviously watching Fowler's hotel. The moment he spotted Fargo, he bolted into an alley between a brewery and a ramshackle boardinghouse.

Fargo sprinted into the street but was immediately impeded by a massive freight wagon lumbering past, sideboards straining. By the time he gained the alley entrance, Doyle was gone. This entire riverfront section of Saint Joseph was a warren of alleys, and Fargo knew that catching Doyle would be like locating a splinter in an elephant's ass.

"The reckoning is coming, woman killer," he muttered quietly as he headed toward the livery in the southern outskirts of Saint Joe.

We got to move full bore. Fargo's own words reverberated in his skull as he paced off the blocks. Pinkerton's thorough, methodical procedures often yielded good results, but Fargo knew that game was no longer worth the candle. Time was the worst enemy now, and slow and steady would *not* win this race.

It was high time to do things Skye Fargo's way.

It was high time to stir up the shit.

By the time he reached the livery, Fargo had sketched out a reckless plan of action—one he dared not reveal to Pinkerton. If he miscalculated, the results could be disastrous—might even save the syndicate instead of bringing it to justice. All depended on Fargo's instincts and some mighty thin evidence.

"Bo, after that showdown with Winslowe and Reece last night, I figured mebbe you skipped town," Septimus greeted Fargo.

"What, without my horse? They always talk who never think."

Fargo crossed to a saddle rack in the tack room and dug in to one of his saddle pockets, looking for his copy of the contract he'd signed with Allan Pinkerton.

Septimus snapped his quirt at a fly. "That-air Sheriff Winslowe, now he ain't 'xactly knowed for bein' no great thinker. But he's a right decent sort. Took guts for him to buck the mayor like he done last night."

"I s'pose," Fargo said absently, still digging.

Septimus's gravelly voice took on a scornful edge. "But Reece . . . actin' all biggity, the blamed fool, and his own daughter layin' there dead."

Septimus paused and his voice softened. "Sure, that gal was secondhand. But I feel powerful bad for all 'em things I said agin her. You can't kill Jack Parsons quick enough to suit *this* child."

Fargo found the contract, folded it, and stuffed it in his hip pocket. "I may yet kill Parsons, old roadster, but he didn't kill Lily."

"You harping on Doyle agin? Fargo, I won't minch the matter: Doyle is too stupid to kill time let alone a woman."

Fargo headed for the wide front door. "I've gone round and round on this before with half the thick skulls in Missouri, you included. Think whatever you please, but keep a sharp eye on my horse, hey?"

"Where you goin'?" Septimus called to his back.

"Crazy. Wanna come?"

But as Fargo emerged into the bright spring sunshine and considered what he was about to do, he half suspected he might indeed be crazy.

Colonel Ambrose Meriwether answered the door almost immediately after Fargo knocked.

"Yes?" he said, curiously eyeing the rough-and-ready type standing on his porch.

"Colonel, we've never met, but I've done a lot of work for the army over the years. The name is Fargo. Any chance I might talk to you on a matter of considerable importance?"

Meriwether wore an immaculate well-tailored uniform with knife-edge creases. The crisp blue elegantly offset his silver hair.

"Fargo?" he repeated. "Skye Fargo, right? Sometimes known as the Trailsman?"

"Among other things."

Meriwether, his face a mask of puzzlement, stood aside and opened the door wider. "Come on in, Mr. Fargo. You don't strike me as the type to make social calls."

Unlike Mayor Reece's house, also located on Enterprise Street, the colonel's home was clean but spartan, with only a few pieces of simple furniture. He directed Fargo to a horsehair-stuffed chair in the front room, seating himself on a wooden chair before a battered kneehole desk covered with papers.

"I'd say you have indeed done some work for the army," he told Fargo. "I recall hearing about an incident up on the Rosebud in the Department of Dakota. Seems the commanding officer and the senior sergeants were killed in a sudden attack by warpath Sioux against a twenty-man mapping expedition. It was down to you and a bunch of snot-nosed recruits who had never fired their weapons before. But you rallied them and got back to the fort with only two additional casualties. All this after the officer in charge ignored your repeated warnings, as contract scout, that an attack was coming. Plenty of newspapers called you a hero."

"That was a hell-buster," Fargo admitted. "But don't forget, I saved my own bacon that day, too. 'Heroes' sell newspapers."

Meriwether smiled. "I suppose. As for me, I spend more time in the map files than I do the saddle. But it seems that a lot of other men survive when Skye Fargo saves his own bacon."

Fargo cleared his throat. "Well, I didn't come here to recite my coups. Colonel, I know why you're here in Missouri. And I'm here today to help prevent the heist of the next U.S. Treasury gold shipment and break up the syndicate behind it."

At this unexpected announcement, Colonel Meriwether's face closed like a book. His eyes slid toward the Henry propped against Fargo's chair, and his right hand inched closer to the flap holster of his service revolver.

Fargo grinned. "No reason to get spooky on me."

"I don't know what you're talking about, Fargo. I've heard of these robberies, of course. But I'm with the Quartermaster Corps—procurement of supplies. I have nothing to do with gold shipments."

"Look, I know all about army oaths, and I won't ask you to tell me when this next express is rolling. But I've never taken an oath in my life and never will. So take a gander at this."

He handed Meriwether the contract. The officer read it, then shuffled through the papers on the desk, comparing the contract to one of them.

"It's Pinkerton's signature, all right," he conceded. "And I knew he was on this case. But his operatives usually conceal their identity. Why are you revealing yours to me?"

"Because of Inge Johanson."

Whatever Meriwether expected, this wasn't it. At first he looked confused. Then his face was transformed by anxiety—and finally guilt. The guilt of a married man in an age when adultery was a prison offense.

"You've knocked the wind out of me, Fargo. You don't strike me as a blackmailer."

Fargo snorted. "I wish it was that piddling."

"Since I'm not at all sure where this is going, why don't you just speak freely?"

Fargo nodded. "Inge also works for Pinkerton."

"She . . . ? So that explains it. I was vain enough to think—"

"That she was really falling in love with you?"

Meriwether flushed slightly. "Yes. I never strayed from my marriage vows in my life until I met that gorgeous, irresistible woman. So she's been watching me all along? That doesn't bother me one bit, but I'm surprised that a morally upright man like Pinkerton would let an employee use sex to catch a supposed thief."

"He wouldn't and he hasn't," Fargo said. "And she isn't watching you, Colonel. She knows all about your past acquittal on charges of payroll theft. And she's building on that in an attempt to frame you for these latest robberies—and murders, I ought to add."

Meriwether stared as if Fargo had announced she was Satan's bride. "Frame me? Come now, Fargo. Pinkerton's agency is famous for never framing evidence to support a client."

"Pinkerton doesn't know a damn thing about what she's up to. She's playing him the same way she's playing you and anyone else wearing trousers."

"This is simply . . . Do you have proof?"

"Have you got a spare tunic hanging in a closet?" Fargo asked.

"Two of them."

"Go search the pockets."

Still looking confused, and a good deal skeptical, Meriwether left the room. He returned a minute later holding a small scrap of paper. Fargo already knew what it said but glanced at it when the colonel handed it to him, his face grim now.

"I've never seen that note before in my life," he swore.

"I've decided to believe that," Fargo assured him.

"Are you suggesting she put it there?"

"I don't have the proof. But I'm pretty damn sure she did. I can vouch for the Pinkerton agent who found it."

Meriwether sank down into the chair and sat in stunned silence.

"Colonel," Fargo probed, "you brought her back here, didn't you? Overnight, I mean?"

He nodded. "Several times. So of course she had the opportunity."

Fargo gestured toward the desk. "And all those papers—telegrams, express schedules and whatnot—she could have learned all she needed to know about routes, time, security for the express runs?"

"Jesus Christ." Meriwether shook his head, trying to shake off this nightmare. "There was one night—I woke up and she wasn't in bed with me. I saw a lamp was burning out here. I— Instead of getting up, I called to her. She came in the bedroom holding a goddamn book of Irish poetry. Told me she couldn't sleep so she was just doing a little reading."

"I'll wager she was *reading*, all right," Fargo said in a sarcastic voice. "Were all your papers just lying out like they are now?"

"No, I lock them in the desk when I turn in. And I hide the key. But frankly, a Pinkerton agent could open this primitive lock with a hatpin."

Meriwether was so humiliated he couldn't look Fargo in the eye. "Fargo, you don't mean she's *running* the gang? I mean, there was at least one robbery before she even came—"

"No, she didn't start the syndicate. She just moved in on it. It's either Mayor Reece or Hardiman Burke she's teamed up with, maybe even both. My money's on Burke because she claims she's seen you and Reece exchange secret messages of some kind."

"Hogwash! Now I know you're right. I only know Reece through her."

Fargo nodded. "Like I said, smart money's on Burke. He and Inge like to take long rides out of town. I'd say that's when they meet with the gang to give them marching orders."

"So you're thinking she identified Burke early on. Did the same thing to him she did to me—used that incredible beauty and intellect and feminine allure to mesmerize him? And because I'm already on record as an accused thief, I'm supposed to take the fall?"

"It all fits," Fargo said. "Fits like a glove. And I've got a strong hunch she means to have a piece of human shit named Kirby Doyle kill Burke, too. Why split the swag any more than she has to?"

"The mastermind," Meriwether said. "The Missouri mastermind. But what about this gang—the actual road agents? Have you got a lead on them?"

Fargo grinned. "You're palavering with a member of the gang right now."

This coaxed a weak, brief smile from Meriwether. "Fargo, you're some piece of work."

"No, sir, the *work* is still ahead for both of us. There's not yet enough evidence to charge her and Burke let alone convict them. And I'm afraid to try and deal Pinkerton in just yet. *He's* in love with Inge, too, though he'd never admit it. I'm worried he might unwittingly tip her off."

"Hell yes, she's dangerous. Talk about a Lorelei . . . Well, you're right. I *can't* tell you when this next gold shipment rolls. But I can tell you that two hundred thousand dollars in gold bars is on the line. And I *can* damn sure authorize some last-minute changes, and whatever we devise, you can rest assured she won't find out about it. I may be a fool, but I'm also a quick study."

Fargo nodded. "Good. That means the syndicate will move on the schedule they already have. We need to cook up a plan to take advantage of that. We've *got* to get them dead to rights."

"Damn straight we will. This beguiling little witch proves one thing: Where money is involved there can be no hypocrisy. Fargo, I'm no weak reed when it comes to pretty girls. But I fell hook, line and sinker for her act—the tortured, sensitive woman who just couldn't resist me."

Fargo nodded and stood up, snatching up his rifle. "Oh, she's good at working that line, all right. Best I've ever seen. But it's got way beyond hypocrisy, Colonel, if I'm right. I think she even ordered the murder of Lily Reece and tried to frame me for it just to get me off this case. Matter fact, I'm going to settle that little matter right now."

16

Fargo's first move after leaving Meriwether's house was to send a message runner to Fowler's hotel room, instructing him to meet Fargo at the livery. He showed up twenty minutes later.

"What's on the spit?" he greeted Fargo.

Fargo made sure Septimus was out of earshot. "I'll be needing a reliable witness," he said. "Kirby Doyle is going to try to knife me, and naturally I'll have to defend myself. You're going to vouch that it was self-defense."

Fargo fended off his friend's questions and reported the conversation with Colonel Meriwether. He emphasized the point about Inge's late-night "reading" session at Meriwether's house.

"It's still not hand-to-God proof," Fowler mused when Fargo fell silent. "But that tears it for me. She never told me or Pinkerton she'd been to his house—that way she couldn't be connected to the planted note supposedly from Lattimer."

Fargo nodded. "We've got to get Doyle out of the mix. I'll be damned if I'm going to keep looking over my shoulder for him. I can't kill him—yet, anyway—because he might turn into key evidence. But that murdering puke pail could do Inge's next bidding at any time. It's time to put ice in his boots and deal him out of the game for a spell. And we have to make sure he's in no shape to rabbit anytime soon."

"You gonna shoot him? A bullet to the kneecap will lay him out good."

Fargo's face turned hard as granite when he glanced toward the stall where Lily Reece had been found. "Nah. It's going to be a little more personal than that. C'mere."

Fargo led him over to the saddle racks and pulled an

obsidian-bladed knife with a bone handle from one of his saddle bags. The hard black volcanic glass was honed razor sharp on one edge only, Indian fashion.

"I traded a sack of sugar to a Cheyenne brave for this. Nobody's seen it but you. You're going to just happen to be passing by Adams Express when Doyle tries to kill me with this."

"The low-down son of a bitch," Fowler said from a dead pan.

"You don't know me. You don't know him. Got it? You're just a law-abiding concerned citizen shocked at such unprovoked violence. You're even gonna run and fetch the sheriff."

"Why, I'm just Jess Singer, a hardworking drummer from Cleveland trying to sell my gimcracks."

Fargo grinned as he tucked the knife inside his shirt. "God bless the salt of the earth. All right, leave ahead of me and head over to Jules Street. With luck we'll catch him in the wagon yard."

Luck was indeed with Fargo—Doyle was in the hoof-packed yard harnessing a team to a flatbed wagon piled high with new lumber. He dropped a tug chain for a moment to drag on a cigarette. When he spotted Fargo crossing the street toward him he flipped the butt away in a wide arc. If spotting the Trailsman had rattled him, the contemptuous sneer on his face masked it well.

Fargo intended to read this man's face and eyes before he unleashed violence on him. Despite his bone-deep conviction that Doyle was Inge's secret minion and a cold-blooded murderer, he wanted proof that at least convinced him if not Pinkerton.

"You tried to break it off inside me, woman killer," Fargo greeted him, "but it didn't work. Now you'll reap the whirl-wind."

Doyle's flat gunmetal eyes were empty as his soul. "You don't know sic 'em, Fargo. You're just another milk-livered crusader. And you're gonna rue the day you coldcocked me in my shed. Like I said—the worm *will* turn."

Fargo didn't see a man in front of him. This was a type, one that choked every frontier settlement like weeds: mean, dirty, lazy, cocksure men who mocked decent society from lidded eyes and surly faces.

"If you're such a rough and deadly son of a bitch," Fargo goaded him, "why am I standing here? Twice you tried to kill me, and when you botched that you couldn't even get me framed. Hell, any white liver can kill a woman. I'd say Inge needs to hire a squaw—you're penny-ante."

Doyle's thin, bloodless lips curled into a sneer and he folded his arms over his chest. "What I do is no say-so of yours, crusader. That's too damn bad about Lily Reece, ain't it? Maybe she shared her pussy one time too many, uh? You know—just maybe whoever the killer was tricked her into opening her door by saying he was you. Now wouldn't that be just the goddamnedest thing?"

Anger suddenly shortened Fargo's breath, but only for a few heartbeats. Experience took over and he willed himself calm. The perfect moment, for Fargo, was when he became both participant and observer at the same time—as he had earlier when the Pukes surrounded him and as he was now.

"That's all I needed to hear," he said almost cheerfully. "I thank you for what you just said. I knew you'd crater. I knew you'd open your filthy sewer one time too many, knew you'd have to goad me. I won't kill you today because I haven't had my full use of you yet. But when I get done with you right now, you'll wish you'd never pulled a knife on me."

Fargo watched his face contract and harden. "You're shit outta luck, crusader. I ain't got a gun *or* knife."

From the corner of one eye Fargo saw John Fowler strolling past—and also keeping a careful lookout on the street. He nodded the go sign and, in the space of a finger snap, Fargo had pulled out the obsidian knife and slashed his own left shoulder with it. For the first time Doyle's face registered fear as Fargo dropped the knife in the packed dirt between them.

Fargo set his heels, alert but deadly calm, making sure he didn't signal his next move with his eyes.

"Let's waltz, woman killer," he said just before he unleashed a powerful uppercut that slammed Doyle's mouth shut, breaking his jaw and making his teeth bite off the tip of his tongue.

The forceful blow instantly unhinged Doyle's knees, but Fargo had no intention of stopping there. Out of sight of most of the street traffic, his left hand held Doyle up by his shirt-front while he savaged his face with his right, hard, straight-arm punches while the image of Lily Reece focused his will.

But a broken jaw and a misshapen face wouldn't stop a ruthless killer.

"John!" Fargo called out, panting for breath. "Is it still clear?"

"Looks good, but hurry up! I see a knot of people coming."

Fargo had noticed that one corner of the wagon yard was pockmarked with ant beds. He dragged the battered, uncon-scious man onto it and dropped him face-first, watching angry red ants swarm the murderer. Now it was time to inflict the injuries that would seriously impede any killer. Fargo twisted Doyle's right arm brutally until it broke at the shoulder socket, snapping it with a sound like green wood splitting.

A sharp-edged rock lying nearby sufficed to smash the bones of Doyle's left hand. Fargo, still breathing raggedly from his exertions, his shoulder seeping blood, grinned when he realized: Unless Kirby Doyle could pull a trigger with his dick, Inge Johanson was minus one paid killer.

"All right, Jess Singer!" he called out to Fowler. "Be a good citizen and run fetch the law!"

"God-in-whirlwinds!" Sheriff Harney Winslowe exclaimed. "Fargo, you call this self-defense? This man's been thrashed near to death. Hell, *is* he dead?"

"I think I hear him moaning, Sheriff," Jess Singer volun-teered.

"Christsakes, help me pull him off them anthills. Fargo, I s'pose he landed on them just by happenchance?"

Fargo made a big show of holding his wounded shoulder and wincing at the pain. "You know, Sheriff, it's all sort of a blur. It happened so fast."

Winslowe grunted as he and the helpful drummer from Cleveland pulled Doyle to safer ground.

"And it just so happens it's Kirby Doyle, huh? The same simple-shit half-wit you claim killed Lily Reece?"

Sheriff Winslowe had shown up toting a .44 caliber North and Savage revolving-cylinder rifle. He seemed uncertain whether to point it at Fargo or not. He looked at the bowler-clad drummer.

"You say you seen what happened?"

"Yessir. I was walking past this wagon yard and I noticed Mr.—Fargo, is it?—Mr. Fargo here talking to this fellow who's now on the ground."

"Were they having what you might call a heated altercation, or was Fargo flat-out knocking him around?"

Jess Singer's earnest moon face was concentrated with the effort to report accurately and fairly. "No, Sheriff, it didn't appear too heated. No voices were raised, and at first I noticed no threatening gestures. Just, all of a sudden like, the gent now on the ground pulled that shiny black knife out and lunged at Fargo."

Winslowe's flat-as-a-skillet face turned toward Fargo, who again winced in pain. "Lunged, huh?"

"Yessir. He tried to cut Fargo's throat, but Fargo twisted aside and got that cut on his shoulder. Then Fargo began retreating—"

"Retreating, huh?" Winslowe cut in skeptically. "Funny you should use just that word. And, Mr. Singer, you say you don't know Fargo?"

"Never saw him before today, Sheriff. I'm with the Stanton Company of Cleveland, purveyors of ladies' notions, and—"

Winslowe waved him silent. "Yeah, ladies' notions. Fargo, you four-flusher. You're lying sure as gumption. I'll give you the busted jaw and beat-up face *if* Doyle jumped you with a knife. But *look* at his damn right arm—it looks like it was cut off and sewed back on backwards! And his left hand is all swole up like a bladder bag. Son, that ain't self-defense. He looks like Viking berserkers worked him over."

"Hell, Sheriff, you can see *I'm* wounded. The man came at me like a pack of wolverines, clearly bent on cutting my throat. Maybe I got a little carried away—"

"He's the one that'll be carried away—after we rake him up. The hell was you doing here anyhow?"

"Why, hell, I just stopped by to ask him if he knew anything at all about what happened to Lily Reece. Next thing I knew, he was trying to put me under."

A pathetic, drawn-out moan escaped Doyle's swollen, ant-bitten lips. He sounded like a dog dying in a ditch.

"Sheriff, I saw all of it," Jess Singer told Winslowe. "If you'd like one of my business cards—"

"You can stick that goddamn card where the sun don't shine. *Both* you four-flushing liars get the hell outta my sight before I shoot you. Fargo, I'll warn you: The pitcher can go once too often to the well. You cross me one more time and I'll slap you in irons!"

"He started it," Fargo said indignantly as both men cleared out. When they were halfway across the street, Fowler muttered, "That was a close shave. But you sure's hell put the wrath on Doyle. He can't even wipe his own ass much less do anything for Inge."

"Yeah, but don't tack up any bunting just yet. I figure trouble is only a fox step away and things will soon be happening ten ways a second. I got a feeling Inge can be dangerous under her own steam, and don't forget Burke. There's a good chance they can harness Lattimer's bunch. From here on out, old son, watch your backtrail and watch it close."

By the evening of that eventful day Fargo received the summons he'd been expecting: a message from Pinkerton to report immediately.

"This Uncle Pete a yours must be a lonely son of a buck," Septimus quipped after relaying the message. "Tell him I'll rent him a stall right next to yours for the price of all these messages."

"I'll pass that along to him," Fargo said as he headed out into the grainy twilight. "Take a care, old-timer, and keep that Colt Army handy."

John Fowler had arrived before him. Pinkerton, as Fargo had expected, was in an awful wax.

"No Inge?" Fargo said casually as he settled into a chair.

"*She's* out doing her job," Pinkerton snapped. "And you two reckless fools are jeopardizing everything she's doing."

Fargo met Fowler's glance before looking at Pinkerton. "How so?"

"Don't come the wide-eyed ingénue with me, Fargo! I just had a bit of supper at the Bluebird Café on Frederick Street. The whole place is buzzing with the story about how the famous Trailsman left feckless Kirby Doyle looking like a side of tenderized meat."

"So what?" Fargo shot back. "Is he a relative of yours?"

Fowler coughed in a belated attempt to cover up a sputter of laughter. Pinkerton turned choleric but only looked at Fargo as if he were something nasty he had just scraped off his shoe.

"Your humor escapes me. *Why* did you beat this man so savagely? Good Lord, Fargo! They say the tip of his tongue is missing!"

Fargo had to be careful here. He couldn't admit that the beating was a safeguard against any future orders Inge might give Doyle. He had no hard evidence that Doyle was working secretly for Inge—and possibly Burke. And despite the things he'd learned from Meriwether and Fowler about the mysterious blonde, there was no hard evidence yet against her, either. In the absence of undeniable proof, and given Pinkerton's infatuation with the woman, the doting old fool would let her in on everything.

"Why? Because he admitted to me that he killed Lily Reece," Fargo replied. "Taunted me with it. I lost my temper."

Pinkerton went a shade paler above his beard. Fargo knew this claim was a stretch, but not by much. Doyle had indeed clearly implied his own guilt.

Pinkerton looked at Fowler. "Did you hear this confession also, John?"

"I did," Fowler lied without effort.

Pinkerton drummed his fingers on the gargantuan desk. "Then why didn't you both go to Sheriff Winslowe and tell him? The Reece murder is his bailiwick, not yours."

"Winslowe?" Fowler said. "That sad sack couldn't catch a cold much less a murderer."

"Damn it!" Pinkerton exploded. "We *have* a case already, an important one! Evidently Sarah—Inge is the only one who realizes that. Why can't you two show the loyalty she has?"

Fargo's eyes cut to Fowler's.

"No need to have a conniption, boss," Fargo said. "We're going to crack this case wide open for you."

"How? Or is it intrusive to ask my *employees* what they're up to?"

"It's like this," Fowler put in. "Fargo and me are caught between the sap and the bark. You want us to wrap this up quick, yet you insist we have to put proof before hunches."

"Of course! That's how modern scientific crime detection works. One goes from inductive evidence to deductive conclusions. You two are engaging in mere fancy, which can coin some wrong ideas."

"We're not trying to sell you a bill of goods," Fargo said. "Your methods are good, Allan, and you've grown rich by getting results with them. But time is nipping at our sitters, and me and John need some leeway here. We both promise you this: The proof you need is coming and mighty damn soon."

"So this is a rebellion, is that it?"

"Just a difference of opinion," Fargo insisted. "We both listened to that stirring speech you gave about how the American experiment could fail if this new monetary system is defeated in favor of gold hoarding. We agree. Just let us follow our instincts."

Pinkerton threw up his hands in disgust. "Even now, as we speak, faithful Inge is working night and day, *following instructions,* not instincts. If you bollix up all her hard work . . ."

He trailed off, at a loss for words, and Fargo again leveled an ironic look at Fowler.

"Yeah, she's some pumpkins," Fargo said.

"The best, and don't you two hotheads forget it. All right then, rebels, follow your 'instincts.' But write this on your pillowcases, both of you: You'd *better* get that proof you promised, and get it before you start shooting. A 'hunch' is not worth a tinker's damn unless it's right."

17

This time Dog Man didn't catch Fargo off guard.

The night began uneventfully enough. Fargo, bone-tired and operating on too little sleep, returned to the livery after leaving Pinkerton's office and shared a can of beans with Septimus. Afterward the old salt broke out his jug and the two men sat on nail kegs passing the liquor back and forth.

"I hear Doyle is in the charity hospital on River Street," Septimus said. "They say he's in so much pain he's drinking laudanum by the bottle. Word is he'll be laid up for weeks."

"I'll have to send flowers," Fargo replied, listening to horses snuffle and make the straw rustle when they moved.

Septimus chuckled. "That ain't the half of it, bo. Our ten-penny sheriff is starting to change his tune about you. He found Doyle's gun belt."

This jerked Fargo out of his lassitude. "Where?"

"He was pokin' around behind the express office. Found it in a covered rain barrel. A fancy nickel-plated Remington. Wood grips, and they was nine notches in one of 'em. The belt buckle's got the initials K.D. on it."

"Be damn," Fargo said.

"That ain't all. They was a fancy pearl necklace and a pair o' gold earrings in the barrel. The mayor says they belonged to Lily, all right. Winslowe's charging Doyle with murder."

"Music to my ears, Dad. But how do you know all this?"

"Straight from the horse's mouth. Mayor Reece come by here to apologize to you."

"Why didn't you tell me sooner, you old coot? You been sitting on this since I came back."

"Ahuh. I spill bad news right away, but I gen'rally save good news till I'm sippin' whiskey."

By now, Fargo knew, Fowler and Pinkerton, too, must have heard the news. And so had Inge and Burke. It would likely make them even keener to put Skye Fargo below the horizon.

"The hull damn town missed it," Septimus said. "But you sized him up right off as a killer. It's easy for a feller to catch him a reputation as a gun-thrower. Back in the land of steady habits, folks are death on bloodcurdlin' tales of pistoleros. But only a few hombres get beyond a reputation to downright fame like you got."

"I'm not all that famous," Fargo gainsaid. "Being famous is safer. Men admire fame but they challenge a reputation—and I get my share of challenges."

"Well, anyhow, whatever the hell you are," Septimus said, "I'm proud as a game rooster to know you."

"Does this mean I'm spoken for?" Fargo quipped, and both men shared a laugh.

"I know this much," Septimus said, wiping his mouth on the back of his hand. "I'm poor as Job's turkey, mebbe, but I'm damn lucky. It's a rare man who lives to be fifty in Missouri, and I'm sixty-two. Looks like I owe Satan twelve years."

By now weariness and rotgut liquor had made Fargo's eyelids feel weighted with coins. He bade the old man good night, grabbed his saddle for a pillow and walked back to the new stall he'd picked out—it would give him the fantods to sleep where Lily had been found dead.

Again, as he quickly tumbled over the threshold into sleep, he reminded himself: Kirby Doyle wasn't the only paid killer in Missouri, and by now Inge had to know that Skye Fargo was a serious threat.

Fargo had no idea how long he'd been asleep, but a warning whiffle from the Ovaro jolted him fully awake in an eyeblink. He rose to his knees, then into a low crouch, skinning back his Colt and thumb-cocking it.

He moved silently to the end of the stall. Septimus had left a single lantern burning, hanging from a crosstree up near the tack room. It was enough light to show Dog Man about twenty feet away.

"Holster that thumb-buster, Fargo," he said in a low voice. "I ain't here to blow out your lamp. We got us a little problem."

"How little?"

"Exactly the size of Jack Parsons. The goddamn love-struck fool has gummed up the works. Stand by for the blast." He stopped near Fargo, trailing a reek of forty-rod. "It's been chappin' his ass ever since you told him Doyle killed that crazy redheaded slut."

"Hell, he damn near laughed in my face when I said it."

"That's just his way. But he knows you been right all along, and he got to stewing on it. Swore he'd curl his toes for him. Anyhow, I come into town tonight to plant my carrot in a little whore I like at Cooter Brown's. Parsons was there, so drunk he was walking on his knees. He heard about Doyle bein' at the charity hospital, and the stupid son of a bitch sneaked in and killed him."

Fargo immediately seized the problem. Despite the fact that Doyle was now a suspect in the murder of Lily Reece, it would be widely assumed that Fargo sneaked into that hospital and finished the job he started.

"We can't afford to let you get tossed in the hoosegow," Dog Man explained. "And if you go into hiding at our camp, there'll be a thousand redneck peckerwoods combing the woods looking to collect the reward that'll be on you. That could bollix up our next heist."

"So what's your big idea?"

"No body, no crime, right? If Doyle just disappears, nobody can say for sure what happened to him."

Fargo thought about it and it made sense. "Well, things are the way they are, that's all. Septimus is passed out drunk by now—he won't miss a conveyance and team. How'd Jack kill him?"

"Hell, who knows? He was blubbering in his goddamn beer when I left him, the nancy. That little whip-crackin' frippet use to get him howling like a dog in the hot moons. He never had pussy that exciting—made him twat simple."

Fargo led the way to the tack room and grabbed an old canvas groundsheet bunched up in a corner. "We'll wrap the body in this after we weight it down with rocks, then tie him tight and dump him way out in the middle of the river. But can we get him out of the hospital without getting caught?"

"It's more like what you call a pesthouse than a hospital. It's down on River Street just past the steamboat landing. Hell, it ain't no bigger 'n a packing crate. But we'll hafta haul Doyle north outta town for a ways before we dump him— too many people around there."

A buckboard sat out behind the livery among the rental conveyances. Fargo led a pair of dray horses outside and the two men threw the harness on the team and hooked up the traces. Fargo climbed onto the board seat and took up the reins, Dog Man lying down in the bed.

Fargo pulled his hat low even though the poor lighting in Saint Joe made it unlikely he'd be recognized. He snapped the reins and they lumbered into motion.

"We're passing the steamboat landing," he told Dog Man about ten minutes later.

The half-breed sat up. "It's that low building up on the knoll to the right. Best go past it and park in them trees—no telling if somebody's found the body. We just might have to plug a law dog or two."

"Put that notion out of your head. We *will* have posses beating the bushes if we shoot a starman."

Fargo pulled over and wrapped the reins around the brake. They stuck to shadows as they crept up on the building. There was a single, open window on the street side. A weak light flickered within. They cat-footed up and peered over the sill.

"Jesus Christ with a wooden dick!" Dog Man whispered hoarsely. "I ain't *even* believing this shit."

The "hospital," obviously unattended at the moment, was merely a single narrow room with five cots lined up. Only one, the cot nearest the window, was occupied. A fat candle burning on a stool beside it revealed a horse blanket sopping with blood. Kirby Doyle lay under it, his throat slashed deep from ear to ear.

"I was hoping Jack might maybe make it look like Doyle cashed in his own chips," Dog Man muttered. "But whoever heard of a man damn near cutting his own head off?"

"Especially," Fargo added, "when he can't even hold a

knife. C'mon, let's haul him out before somebody comes along."

Fortunately, none of the blood had dripped onto the floor or the cot. They left the blanket on the body and wrestled it out to the buckboard, heaving Doyle into the bed like a side of beef. Fargo drove the conveyance north until the raucous noise and oily glow of River Street gave way to shape-changing shadows and a few dilapidated shanties. The broad, moonlit expanse of the Missouri River reflected ribbons of moonlight here and there.

"There's a skiff," Fargo said, tugging the left rein and guiding the buckboard onto the grassy bank. "We'll have to get him away from shore or steamboat wash might turn the body up."

They gathered rocks and rolled them up with the body in the groundsheet, tying the grisly package tight at both ends with sisal rope Fargo had grabbed at the livery. But when they were untying the skiff from its mooring post, a dog started yowling.

From a nearby shack, the unmistakable sound of hammers being pulled back froze both men in place. "Who goes there?" shouted a belligerent voice. "Sing out, damn you, or I'll let moonlight through you!"

"We're butternut guerrillas!" Dog Man roared out, using a common name for the Pukes. "Here's a taste of what you'll get, cheese dick, if you get frisky with *us*!"

He raised his sawed-off and triggered both barrels together, blowing the stovepipe chimney off the shack and sending a deafening, crack-booming explosion echoing out across the river. The barking ceased instantly, replaced by a frightened whimpering.

The voice from the shack shed its belligerence. "Katy Christ, boys, hold your powder! I'm for slavery! I figgered you was somebody robbing my trotline!"

"We're headhunters!" Dog Man called back. "Just stay inside and pipe down, and you'll live to see the sunrise."

The two men heaved the body into the skiff and Fargo took the oars, rowing them out toward midstream. It was a chilly, clear night, a far-flung explosion of stars dotting the sky like a million sparks. Sound carried easily over water, and on the far bank he heard someone with a banjo picking out the notes to "Wood Ticks in My Johnny."

When they were well out in deep water, the current starting to fight them, Fargo and Dog Man plopped the corpse splashing into the water. It sank quickly, a string of popping bubbles marking its descent.

"A few days from now," Dog Man remarked, "he'll look like suet pudding."

As Fargo tacked the skiff around to head back to shore, Dog Man suddenly tossed back his head and wolf-howled at the moon. "Blood, guts, deception and death! Another damn good night in Misery, Fargo. Think of all them pus-guts in town missing all this fun."

"The pathetic fools," Fargo said in a deadpan voice.

"Don't think," Dog Man added, "that just 'cause I helped save your skin tonight it means I trust you."

"Trust everybody," Fargo said, "but always cut the cards."

"'At's right."

Dog Man raised his scattergun for emphasis. "One part a me says, 'Dog Man, Fargo's on the level and he's just the boy to get you to safety in Mexico.' But another part says, 'Dog Man, that son of a bitch is sailing under false colors. You may have to put fire in his belly yet.'"

18

The bulldog edition of next morning's *Saint Joseph Pioneer* carried a front-page headline that screamed its indignation:

ACCUSED WOMAN KILLER DISAPPEARS!!!

The accompanying story again prominently mentioned Fargo's role in putting Kirby Doyle in the hospital. But it stopped short of linking him to the mysterious disappearance. Instead, Sheriff Harney Winslowe was roundly criticized for his decision that Doyle was "too dang banged up to require a guard."

"Poor Winslowe," John Fowler sympathized as he tossed the newspaper aside. "But I don't see how you had any other choice, Fargo. A man can't pop over too many bad guys from a jail cell."

"The way you say," Fargo agreed. "Jack Parsons cost me a lot of sleep last night, that tangle-brained fool. But if he hadn't done for Doyle, some vigilante eventually would have. Winslow had to know that when he left Doyle unguarded. I give him credit for saving the taxpayers the cost of a trial and hanging."

"There's that," Fowler said. "When I was packing a star, there were a few prisoners who, ah, tried to escape before I got 'em back to town."

"So don't worry about 'poor Winslowe.' The newspaper bawl babies may fake outrage, but the folks who elect the sheriff know Doyle is most likely a worm castle by now. And Winslowe's a hero to them."

The two men were enjoying a quick bite of lunch at the

Hog's Breath. They had just finished a long strategy session at the home of Colonel Ambrose Meriwether. Two plans had been worked out: one for tossing a net around Lattimer's gang, the other for obtaining the crucial evidence needed to nab the brains behind the express-robber operation.

"I'm glad we finally know the next gold shipment rolls through this area tomorrow," Fowler said between bites of Katy's delicious beef and biscuits. "But we still don't know exactly where and when. Anyway, that means Lattimer will most likely send for you today. If you're going to make medicine with Inge, you'd best shake a leg."

Fargo nodded. "No bout adoubt it, pard. I just hope she takes the bait."

"She's the type to figure percentages and angles. She'll take it when she sees how much more of the swag she'll get."

Fargo didn't look so sure. "She's not just smart—she's dangerous. You know damn well she's got a hideaway gun and the will to use it. She scares me more than Dog Man does. If she even *suspects* I'm running a con on her, she'll kill me dead as a dried herring."

"Horse shit. She's use to duping men like me—poor slobs who go all giddy when she flashes that up-and-under look of hers. Women can't job Skye Fargo, but this one *thinks* she can. That's the rock she'll split on—overconfidence."

Fowler sopped up the last of his gravy, scowling. "What gripes my ass is this sittin' on my pratt while you take all the arrows."

"Balls. You've got maybe the hardest job of all—you've got to convince Pinkerton to play his part when the time comes. He trusts your judgment more than mine."

"Christ, I hope he does. If I bollix it up, he'll run straight to her, and she'll bat them beautiful blue eyes. And he'll feel his dick move and spill everything. And that'll row you right up Salt River."

"Good times ahead, hey? Well, I never figured to live forever. If that little vixen rubs me out, tell Septimus he can have my horse."

"Can I have your Henry?"

Fargo narrowed his eyes. "You just said no woman can job Skye Fargo."

Fowler grinned. "People say a lot of lying shit when a man's about to die."

"You *do* know how to wound a woman's vanity, Skye Fargo. After your last visit I'd hoped you would be back sooner."

Fargo stepped into the luxurious hotel room and laid his hat on a marble letter stand by the door. His eyes raked approvingly over Inge. She wore a simple, form-flattering black dress with cream lace cuffs. The pale blond hair was pinned and netted under a snood. All that was missing, Fargo told himself, was a halo.

"Never mind those bedroom eyes—for now," she said on a musical laugh. "I have an appointment with Hardiman Burke soon."

"Good," Fargo said. "Let's kill him."

If he meant to shock her out of her aplomb, he failed.

"I'd like to," she riposted lightly as if picking up on a joke. "He's a tiresome man who wears so much cologne he attracts flies."

"Straight-arrow," Fargo said. "Let's kill him. You don't need that old poncy anymore. I killed Kirby Doyle last night to get him off the books. Tomorrow, as soon as I help the gang get the bullion, I'm gonna kill all three of them, too, and save us a hundred thousand in payout to them. With Burke out of the way, it's just me and you and two hundred thousand in gold."

Even now the sweet, attentive, perplexed look on her face showed no strain. Fargo recalled that indignant, high-minded speech she had made in Pinkerton's office. One line was definitely true: *I am of an individual and contrary nature.*

"Why, Skye Fargo," she scolded. "Have you been drinking?"

"No. But I been *thinking*—thinking a lot about the two of us in that fancy bed, climbing all over each other. And I want more of it—plenty more of it. I want you for my woman."

John Fowler might not be a ladies' man, Fargo knew. But he was dead-on about Inge and her cocksure belief that all men lived in her pocket. She could bewitch any man with her siren song, and why should Skye Fargo be the exception?

"No man ever took me as completely as you did," she

replied, working that little husk into her voice. "But I'm at a loss for words. Why don't you just keep talking?"

"I saw all of it in just a few days. With your intelligence you spotted Burke as the ringleader right off. You made him fall in love with you, then told him you knew what he was up to. He was eager to deal you in if it meant keeping you. He had already hired Kirby Doyle to put the fear of God in Lattimer's bunch, but you started using Doyle on the side for your own purposes. After this job tomorrow, and Lattimer's bunch was paid off, Kirby Doyle was to kill Burke."

"My goodness," she said, two scarlet points appearing in her prominent cheeks, "your mind *has* been active."

"But I say why pay Lattimer and his greasy outfit a damn thing either? I can pop them over with three quick head shots while they're drooling over all that color. That's an extra hundred thousand for me and you. We can disguise that bullion in wooden crates and ship it with us on a train to New Orleans or Boston or any damn place you want to live. Meantime, thanks to your brilliance, the law will be focused on Colonel Meriwether."

Fargo tugged on the bloody fringes of his shirt. "I can shuck these buckskins for swallowtails and a topper. We'll get hitched and live like Rockefellers."

She was rapt with attention, sniffing a great opportunity here, but Fargo saw the predatory caution in her eyes. His proposal wildly increased her share of the profits—especially after she got her use out of Skye Fargo and killed him, too. But this was no woman for reckless action—only cold, precise calculation.

"What about Lily Reece?" she asked bluntly.

"I don't follow."

"She was killed on the same night that we made love. Kirby Doyle did it, and you have theorized that I employ—employed—Doyle. That means you believe I ordered her death, doesn't it? To frame you and get you off the case? How could you possibly trust a woman like me if you believe all that?"

That was exactly what Fargo believed, but the lie was easy. "You didn't order it. Doyle was getting even with me for threatening him, for knocking him out and searching his shack. A clash of stags. You couldn't have sent me to prison—there's been something special between us from day one. I knew it for sure when we made love. We belong together."

"Of course it was special," she said in a low, seductive voice. "And as for our being together . . ."

As Fargo had spoken, she had gradually edged closer to a small reticule sitting on a mahogany table. Fargo knew why and felt his stomach twist into a knot—now came the moment of truth. It was a roll of the dice, and snake eyes meant that he would die.

In a moment she had it out and pointed at him: a two-shot ladies' muff gun, and its compact size belied its deadly large caliber. Fargo suddenly felt fear itching like a new scab.

"You've just made quite a confession of your recent activities," she told him. "One tug on that velvet rope beside you will bring a porter up here, and I can send him for the sheriff. Or . . ."

She clicked back both hammers. "I could just kill you now for forcing your way in and trying to rape me. You know that no jury in the West would find me guilty."

"Jury? It wouldn't even get that far. Your word would close the case."

She nodded, sending him an enigmatic smile. "Lattimer wouldn't like it, of course, because of his fears about getting safely to Mexico. And Hardiman and I *want* his gang to reach Mexico—we need those three potential witnesses against us out of the picture. What to do?"

"We do it my way," Fargo said. "The easy and profitable way. Four bullets is all it'll cost me to get Burke and the others off your back. And there's something else you need to consider: With me dead, what stops Lattimer's bunch from taking *all* that gold? Kirby Doyle isn't around now to keep those jackals in line."

"I confess, Skye, that weighs on me terribly."

She suddenly lowered the hammers and put the gun away. "But I made up my mind minutes ago. You're too clever a man not to have noticed I was reaching for a gun, and you could easily have stopped me. But you didn't. Only a man who loves me could have shown such forbearance in the face of death."

Vanity, Fargo thought. The fact that no man had ever resisted her. The sure and certain knowledge that her beauty, charm and powers of seduction placed her above the law and even gave her the brutal confidence to order the killing of Lily Reece—that overconfidence, as Fowler had divined, was the rock she had split on.

"I've had enough beautiful women to fill a train station," Fargo replied. "But you're the first I've ever fallen for."

"And I love you. We'll do it your way, Skye."

A trio of knocks on the door wiped the angelic smile from her face.

"It's Burke," she said in an urgent whisper. "We're meeting with Lattimer for the final instructions. Hide in the bedroom until we leave. But come back in about two hours. You and I have final plans to make, but Lattimer will be sending for you soon, so don't tarry."

She stretched up on tiptoes and brushed his lips with hers.

"Two hours," Fargo promised before he snatched up his hat and headed for the bedroom door. "And then we'll settle this deal for good."

19

As arranged, John Fowler had waited at his hotel until Fargo reported the outcome of his meeting with Inge. Fargo used the rest of the two hours to stock up on food as Lattimer had ordered.

However, he didn't bother taking the horseshoes Lattimer's gang had given him to a blacksmith for new forgings, knowing they would never be needed. Instead, he borrowed some old horseshoes from Septimus and tossed them in a leather bag—Lattimer had too much on his mind to bother inspecting them right away.

Inge was waiting when he returned to her room, all efficient and ruthless businesswoman now.

"By now that hideous lout Lattimer has no doubt sent word to you to join them," she explained. "But we can't kill Burke up here—we still need him for a bit. I'll make sure he's at his house tomorrow evening. I recommend your knife—he has neighbors close by."

The two of them shared a chintz sofa in the sitting room of her suite. Fargo sipped from a crystal tumbler filled with single-malt scotch, wishing it was a cold beer.

"It'll be a pleasure to kill that windbag," Fargo assured her. "But you didn't tell me about the gold yet. I can't kill Lattimer, Parsons and Dog Man until after we've hauled it to safety. Two hundred thousand in gold bars is a helluva pile, and by myself it'll be a mort of work."

"By now Lattimer and his men are taking two stolen farm wagons and hiding them in the woods near the spot of the robbery. Burke has a large carriage house behind his home. You'll all haul the gold there after dark with bales of hay to cover the gold. The wagons will be left there unloaded. In the past Burke has then shipped it, in smaller quantities, to several buyers."

"So Burke will pay them off in gold when they make the delivery?"

She nodded. "You'll have to kill the gang once you're all outside of town, then return to kill Burke. You won't be able to carry the gang's share of the gold on your horse, so pick a good spot to hide it until we can get back to it. I'll make sure Burke's door is unlocked and I'm there to . . . distract his attention."

"With Burke dead we need some plan to get that gold out of his carriage house pretty damn quick."

"Of course. After killing him we will immediately drive the farm wagons to a room I've rented near the end of Frederick Street. It's dark as a coal bin there at night, and the room has a private entrance off a rear alley. It'll take some time, and we must be quiet, but I can keep watch while you take the bars inside."

Fargo grinned and stroked her satiny cheek. "Don't worry. It'll be done by sunrise. There's one thing I never did quite savvy: Why did Burke give me the nod when Lattimer decided to hire me? He must have cleared it."

She gave him a coy smile. "Because I told him to. I also told him you were working for Pinkerton right alongside me. You know, keep your enemies close and all that? He agreed with me that if we wanted to outwit the Trailsman, we'd have to know his every move. Besides, I knew Pinkerton was bound and determined to hire you, and it would have looked suspicious if I tried to dissuade him."

"I get it," Fargo added. "Both of you counted on the fact that Kirby Doyle would kill me before I learned too much."

She blushed charmingly. "Well, I'm certainly glad he wasn't man enough to do it. I—"

She suddenly paused, watching Fargo carefully. A prickle of alarm moved up his spine at the new, hard glint in her eyes. "What's wrong?"

"Excuse me. I just thought of something. I'll be right back."

She stood up and went into the bedroom. Fargo didn't like the sudden transformation that had come over her face. And he liked it even less when she came out with the two-shot derringer aimed at his vitals.

"You filthy bastard," she bit off in a barely controlled voice.

Fargo sat up straighter, his pulse quickening. "I don't get it."

"*I'm* the one who didn't get it—until now. I don't know how I missed it earlier today, and you repeated it just now. I'm going to kill you, Fargo."

"All right, but can't you at least enlighten me before you do it?"

"Oh, you're a fine actor yourself. But you made one stupid mistake—you mentioned the exact figure of two hundred thousand dollars. *I* know that because I snooped through Meriwether's classified papers. But how could you have known it? Even Pinkerton doesn't know that."

Fargo felt a bead of perspiration roll out of his hair and across his forehead. Of all the lunkheaded mistakes . . .

"Look, lady, you're nerve-frazzled, that's all. I've got a bar-key, remember? I went into his house."

She shook her head. "No, you didn't mention that, and you would have if it was true. He told you in person, and that means I'm being set up. Good-bye, Skye Fargo. You really *were* the best lover I ever had, and that part, at least, I'm going to miss."

Something crashed hard into the door, distracting her for a fractional second, and Fargo suddenly rolled onto the floor fast even as the gun spoke its deadly piece. Another crash, and this time the door banged inward.

"Drop it!" Fowler barked.

But Inge had one shot left and she spun a half turn toward the door. Before she could fire, the Remington bucked in Fowler's hand, and Inge let out a sharp little yip of shock when the muff gun flew out of her hand.

Pinkerton stepped in behind Fowler holding the tubular stethoscope he had used to listen through the door. Colonel Ambrose Meriwether moved in behind him.

"Well, no shit," Fargo said in a disgusted voice as he pushed to his feet. "A second or two later and my toes would be pointing toward the sky."

"The lock is too modern," Fowler said, still covering Inge. "The bar-key didn't work. Thank God Allan's got beefy shoulders."

Pinkerton seemed in a state of shock as he watched the defiant beauty. "Sarah, I still can't believe what I just heard. You talked about cold-blooded murder as if you were trading recipes."

"Spare me the sanctimony, you old fool! All your noble claptrap about saving America . . . If I had spread my legs for you just once you'd have become my partner in crime and murdered infants if I told you to."

"Two of the men in this room have already had you. Let's make it a quartet," Fowler suggested hopefully.

She sent him a cunning look. "I'll screw you into a slight limp if you kill these three—and split a fortune with you."

"If I knock Fargo out will that earn me one quick poke?"

"Belay that filth, John," Pinkerton scolded. "We have arrest powers from the government on this case. Go find Burke and cuff him."

He was still staring at the woman who had betrayed his—and his country's—trust and made a fool of him. "Your looks and charm won't work this time. You are implicated in serious federal charges that include the murder of soldiers. You won't hang, of course—the government has yet to execute a woman because quaint notions of chivalry make it difficult for many to admit women are capable of abject evil. But you'll likely spend the rest of your life in a women's penitentiary."

"Don't be so sure. If there's one man in authority there"—she gave Fargo a sour look—"besides you, Skye, I'll escape."

"Maybe," Fargo suggested, "Colonel Meriwether could use his position to shave a little time off your sentence. Tell us the where and when for tomorrow's heist."

She looked at the colonel. "How *much* time, Ambrose?"

"Substantial cooperation in other federal trials," he replied, "has led to reductions between two and five years."

Her eyes, two hard blue gems now, fastened on Fargo again. "Skye, you damn fool! You're going to regret this later. We could have done everything just as you pretended to plan it."

"I'll have one regret for sure, lady," he said. "That we

only went to bed once before you were arrested. Women like you don't come along too often."

"Thank God," Pinkerton muttered.

She ignored her former boss, but Fargo's compliment coaxed a smile out of her. She looked at Meriwether.

"The strike will be tomorrow afternoon as soon as the express coach reaches Mulberry Valley about fifteen miles north of Saint Joseph. Lattimer plans to attack from the screening timber to the west. He knows there will be no military escort."

Pinkerton looked at Fargo. "You'd better join them now, Skye."

"Hell," Fargo replied, "we know where they'll be and we've bagged the leaders. Let's just go arrest them."

"That's my preference, too. But Colonel Meriwether informs me that the government wants the strongest possible case, and that means we nab them in the heat of the act. The evidence may be inadequate to prosecute them for the earlier robberies."

"Pile on the agony," Fargo complained.

"I'm afraid so, Skye. For God's sake be careful, but remember—we need at least one man taken alive to expedite this trial."

Fargo hailed the camp and rode in to discover only Dog Man waiting for him. The half-breed explained that Parsons and Lattimer had remained to the north, camped with the wagons and teams hidden in the thick pine woods overlooking Mulberry Valley.

"I still ain't made up my mind about you," Dog Man confided as they rode out in silver moonlight, a knife-edge of chill slicing through them each time the wind gusted.

"Does your mother know you're out?" Fargo retorted. "If I was with the law, the net would be tossed over all three of you by now."

"Maybe. But that ain't all that's biting at me. I'm just wondering why a slick case like Skye Fargo would settle for ten thousand while the rest of us get three times that. Lattimer never planned to tell you this, but we're hauling in two hundred thousand dollars tomorrow."

Fargo whistled, then did some quick ciphering. "After this buyer in Galveston does a twenty percent knockdown, you three will get about twenty-three thousand three hundred dollars apiece after I'm paid. Yeah, I'm getting the crappy end of the stick, but you dealt me into the game late. Besides, if I do a good job getting us to Mexico, maybe each of you could chip in an extra thousand or so."

"That don't seem too unreasonable," Dog Man admitted.

The clear moonlight and smooth stage road made it easy to lope their mounts, and they arrived at the latest camp in just over an hour. At first, Jude Lattimer was all rattles and horns as he tied into Fargo.

"Christ Almighty, long-shanks! Where the hell you been—bust your leg in a badger hole? Hell, I sent word to you hours before sundown."

"Ain't you in a fine pucker?" Fargo said as he poured himself a cup of coffee.

"Pucker? God's trousers! I'm savage as a meat ax! Me 'n' Jack coulda used some help with these damn wagons and horses."

"Hell, I wasn't just barking at a knot. It took time to get horseshoes made at two different smithies. And with all them damn pilgrims stocking up for the spring jump-off, I had to scrounge for the grub."

"You want a hankie, Gertrude?" Jack Parsons barbed. "We had to shoot it out with a stubborn hoe-man to get that second wagon."

But Fargo quickly realized that all three men were in a festive mood at the prospect of tomorrow's haul. Dog Man tossed back his head and howled at the moon. "Black your boots, boys. We're goin' on a tear!"

"Break out that oil of gladness, Dog Man," Parsons spoke up. "Tonight we get corned!"

Fargo noticed that, since throat-slashing Kirby Doyle, Jack Parsons seemed to have gotten over his *"amour fou"* for Lily Reece.

"Boys, I can't hardly wait for Mexico," he called out. "Won't be long now. Featherbeds, boiled shirts, twenty-five-cent seegars, pretty senyoreeters in them red petticoats . . .

Moses on the mountain! I might even get me one a them clawhammer coats like Burke wears."

He took a long pull on the whiskey and passed the bottle to Fargo. The four men huddled around a blazing fire pit. The gang were a long way from their last shave, and Parsons's wild thatch of hair looked like it had been brushed with the rough side of a buffalo's tongue.

"Hell," Parsons added in a jubilant tone, "the way American money stretches in Mexico? We're gonna rise so high that when we shit we ain't gonna miss *no*body!"

"All them yacks and yahoos out there," Dog Man pitched in, "toeing the God line and herniatin' theirselves for three hunnert a year, wrapping their leg around the same old sow every night—shit! They ain't nothing but drops of piss in a cesspool."

"Damn straight," Parsons approved. "Say, I even palaver some beaner talk, boys. *Copas gratis para todos!* Savvy that, Fargo?"

"Sure. 'Free drinks for everyone.' "

"You talk Mexer?" Lattimer demanded.

"I picked up some on my trips down there."

"You *are* a good man to take along," Lattimer said. "We'll have to watch ourselves down there, boys. Them greasers can't afford too many guns, but they love their blades—even the women carry 'em. Christsakes, don't say nothing 'bout their ma or pa, and *don't* insult their manhood—them beaners hold a grudge till it hollers mama. Ain't that right, Fargo?"

"Right as rain, Jude. I tend to cinch up my lips when I'm in a cantina down there. A man of few words seldom has to take any back."

"Speaking o' Mexer women, Jude," Dog Man said in a sly tone, "now that you're almost rich, why'n't you grow some a them Piccadilly Weepers? You know, them long, hanging sideburns? You can cover up that ugly scar and get you a mistress. I hear them Mex honeys like to work it all night long. Maybe Jack can even find him one likes to crack a bull-whip in bed."

But Parsons was in too good a mood to take offense. "How 'bout it, Fargo?" he said. "A pocketful of rocks and plenty of them twirling chiquitas to spend it on. No more shit jobs for the army, chum."

"I'm gonna miss all of it," Fargo said with mock solemnity. "The weevil-infested hardtack, the sore testicles, drinking my own piss—"

"No joshing?" Lattimer cut in. "You drank your own piss?"

"Hey, when you're eating boiled buckskin for supper you need a beverage to wash it down."

Drunken laughter greeted this. But silence set in afterward, each man alone with his thoughts while sparks spiraled up out of the fire pit. Fargo felt uncomfortable and even a little guilty. He had infiltrated this hard-bitten group under a cloak of suspicion and had gradually gained acceptance even from the surly Parsons. They were unapologetic murderers and thieves and it had to be done, but somehow it felt unmanly and dishonest to pretend you were an enemy's friend. He would be glad when tomorrow was over—assuming it turned out as planned.

However, the next turn in the conversation forcefully reminded him what these men truly were.

"I been thinking on something, boys," Lattimer said. "Now that Jack has croaked Kirby Doyle, why should we give Burke and that stuck-up bitch *any* of the swag? They'll both likely be together when we haul the bullion to Burke's place. I say we just kill both of 'em and sweeten the pot."

Dog Man laughed and slapped his thigh. "Jude, I was trying to work up to that suggestion myself. We can't haul all that gold with us, but we can hide half someplace safe. Eventually things'll cool off around here and we can come back for it."

"Chappies, I'm with you till the hubs fall off," Parsons chimed in enthusiastically.

"Wha'd'ya say, Fargo?" Lattimer demanded.

"I've heard of this hombre Hardiman Burke," Fargo replied. "I don't know what bitch you're talking about, but neither one of them ever bought me a beer. Sure, let's do it. But I get a bigger share than ten thousand, right?"

"Only fair," Lattimer said. "Matter fact, you get us to the Rio Grande safe and we'll split the whole kitty four ways."

"The bitch," Dog Man said, "is Inge Johanson."

"*Kiss* my ass!" Fargo exclaimed, feigning surprise. "Yeah, you can't be in town and miss her. *She's* in it?"

"Yeah," Parsons said, "and it sure is a goddamn shame, us four hightailing it out of Saint Joe without rippin' some poon off that highfalutin slut. Her sippin' on brandy sours and fartin' through silk, and she's as evil and low-down as us."

"It's settled," Lattimer said, rolling into his blanket. "We'll kill Burke. Then we'll each have a whack or two at blondie before we kill her. Now turn in, alla yous. We got a big day tomorrow and a long, hard haul after that."

20

The following morning, after a spartan breakfast of biscuits spread with bacon grease, Jude Lattimer gathered his men around him.

"All right, boys, let's get a few things straight. Burke claims the government wants this to look like a passenger run, not a gold shipment. So there'll be only two men riding with this coach, the driver and the messenger. Both men are likely to be dead shots, so we don't want a frolic—just a quick slaughter. I want the soles of their feet showing to the world before they even hear the gunshots."

He swept one arm out, indicating the thick pine woods covering the ridge where they'd camped.

"For Christsakes, *don't* shoot wild and hit one of their team horses. We want to drive that coach up here into cover and then kill the horses. The coach will be missed when it doesn't make the way station at Honey Creek. But with the coach and team nowhere to be found, we get extra time to haul the gold out of this area."

Fargo felt a nervous stirring in his stomach. If he didn't prevail at this point he could end up shot to a sieve. But it was crucial to saving lives down below.

"Hold up a minute, Jude," he cut in. "You're not saying we should kill the driver and messenger *before* we stop the coach?"

"Hell yes, that's what I'm saying. We have to show ourselves to stop the coach, and that means getting close enough for us to get plugged."

"Bad idea," Fargo insisted. "I say we stop the coach first."

Three sets of hard, suspicious eyes bored into him.

"Just why would we do that?" Lattimer demanded.

"Don't stare at me, boys—stare down at that valley floor. I mean it, look at it real close."

Fargo waited until they did. "That valley floor is flat as a pancake and that stage road smooth from being graded by the army. It stretches on, straight as a pike, for ten more miles to the way station."

"If you wander near a point, Fargo," Parsons said impatiently, "feel free as all hell to make it."

"The very moment we kill the driver," Fargo said, "he drops the reins and the team leaders, spooked by gunshots and free reins, will panic and run. In terrain like this, with nothing to slow them, it'll take us miles to catch them. That's valuable time we lose. I've scouted every damn part of this area—the trees thin out only two miles east of here and there's farms scattered around. That means witnesses we ain't got time to kill."

Fargo pointed to the wagons and the dray teams waiting behind the screening timber. "Besides, we can't be hauling those rigs all over Robin Hood's barn. That means we lose more valuable time driving the coach back to this spot. And those horses will be blown in from the hard run and likely to sull on us. We could end up getting caught before we can crack the transport safe and get the gold loaded."

"Hell, Jude, all that shines," Dog Man said. "We spooked the team on that first job we done, remember? We was able to shoot them in the traces, but that posse damn near caught us when we wasn't able to hide the coach."

Lattimer pulled at his chin. "Yeah . . . yeah, Fargo does make sense. But damn it all, what choice we got? Fargo, these won't be the usual expressmen with chicken guts, the kind that split when you say hawk. These bastards will have orders to shoot us the moment we show."

Fargo pointed toward the brass-frame Henry poking out of his saddle scabbard. "I can make them go puny," he said confidently, "with just a few good shots."

"Why not let Fargo have first crack at it his way?" Dog Man suggested. "If he botches it, we'll just do it by your plan. Can't hurt to try."

Lattimer's bone-chip eyes studied Fargo for a full ten seconds. "Yeah, all right. Best to save all the time we can. But if you got a fox play in mind, Fargo, I'll guarandamntee it won't work. All three of us are watching you like a cat on a rat."

The morning dragged by, one man always keeping watch with field glasses while the rest smoked, played cards, and talked excitedly of the easy days coming in Mexico. The valley road was nearly deserted. Around ten o'clock a one-horse gig flashed by below; about an hour later Fargo watched a colorful drummer's wagon lumber past, covered with gilt scrollwork and brightly painted scenes.

It was still Fargo's turn on watch when a Concord coach pulled by a team of six big, strong Cleveland bays entered the west pass into the valley.

"Hop your horses, boys!" he sang out. "Here comes the gravy!"

The coach, leather side curtains drawn tight, was making good time across the flat stretch. The driver—whom Fargo knew was a highly skilled army sharpshooter in mufti—repeatedly snapped the standard coach whip, a five-foot hickory stick with a twelve-foot buckskin lash.

He shifted the field glasses on to the skinny messenger rider and grinned when he spotted the familiar moon face. So John Fowler had wangled his way into the action after all?

"All right, Fargo," Lattimer said as he forked leather. "Let's see this fancy shootin' a yours."

Fargo knew this was another risky part of the plan. In order to spare the lives of Fowler and the driver, it had to appear as if they were scared into submission. But if they surrendered too easily, the gang would sniff the trick and blast Fargo to chair stuffings before escaping.

The Trailsman took up his Henry and stretched out in a perfect prone position, digging in his left elbow. He locked the long-barreled repeater into his shoulder socket, worked the lever, and drew a careful bead. The crack of the Henry echoed out across the valley as the driver's hat hopped off his head.

Fargo didn't let up, levering and firing with nonstop precision. His second shot snapped the popper off the whip, his third snapped the hickory in half. A fourth severed one of the reins, a fifth blew Fowler's double-ten from his hands.

This amazing display of marksmanship took mere seconds. Now Fargo bellowed, in a voice powerful enough to fill the valley: "That's just a sample, boys! Halt that coach *now* or the next two bullets will be head shots!"

The driver pressed his foot on the brake and called to the leaders, soothing them to a halt.

"Jesus Christ and various saints!" Parsons exclaimed. "Fargo, that was circus shooting! I never seen the like!"

"Them two galoots are shittin' their drawers!" Lattimer glouted. "C'mon, boys. Let's ride down and get ahold a that damn team before we kill them two. Watch both of 'em close in case they nerve up."

Fargo joined his companions, riding on the left flank. They were within perhaps twenty yards of the coach when the driver sang out: "Up and on the line!"

Fargo tugged left rein and peeled away, shucking out his Colt. Both doors of the coach slapped open and uniformed army sharpshooters boiled out, Spencer carbines cracking the moment they hit the ground.

"It's a trap! Pull foot!" Lattimer bellowed, his face draining white.

All three road agents reversed their dust and headed back up the ridge full chisel. The sharpshooters, following orders to the letter, poured lead into the fleeing men's horses in hopes of taking live prisoners. Lattimer and Parsons managed to swing their legs wide and avoid being pinned under their falling mounts. Dog Man, however, was a beat too slow and ended up trapped under his horse, unable to use his weapons.

Lattimer and Parsons instantly realized that Fargo had planted the Judas kiss on them. Knowing they faced hanging or a firing squad, they vented all their rage on Fargo, opening up on him with a vengeance.

Fargo, bullets whiffing the air all around him, figured it was too late for finesse. His first shot penetrated Lattimer's right eye, his second drilled Parsons straight through the pump. Before either man hit the ground, several Spencer slugs ripped into each one for good measure.

"Cease fire!" roared the soldier up on the box. "They're stew meat now, lads!"

John Fowler sprinted up the slope to join Fargo as he knelt beside Dog Man.

"Any chance—you gents—might get this dead horse off me?" the half-breed said, hissing gasps punctuating his words.

With Fowler and the soldier in charge of covering the prisoner, Fargo pulled Dog Man free when the troopers heaved the horse up a few inches. Both of Dog Man's legs looked like giant broken matchsticks.

He looked at Fargo and managed a nervy little grin. "I knew you was six sorts of trouble, Fargo, but I still like you, you devious son of a bitch."

"We ain't swapping spit, Dog Man, but I admire you, too. You had a couple good chances to kill me but didn't. Your mistake, huh?"

"Wish you'd shoot me right now. All Indians fear the white man's rope—worst way to die."

Fargo leaned closer and lowered his voice. "You might not die, old son, if you play your hand smart. The government wants at least one of the gang to testify against the others. When the prosecutor grills you, hold out until he promises you life in prison."

Dog Man, face twisting in pain, nonetheless perked up. "Shit yeah. I might even escape. And if I don't, least I won't hafta eat my own cooking no more."

After the soldiers hauled Dog Man off to the coach, Fowler looked at Fargo. "Skye, that 'breed murdered soldiers. You know he's gonna try to 'escape' before he gets into civilian custody, don't cha? Broken legs and all? Or so the report will read. Besides, his pards are buzzard bait now. Inge has already signed a full confession implicating Burke, so nobody needs Dog Man's testimony."

Fargo nodded. "Sure, he'll be shot to rag tatters. No skin off my ass. But I didn't have the heart to tell him, Constable. Like I told our lovely blond partner: Hope is a waking dream."

On the second day after "the Great Die-up," as Missouri newspapers had dubbed the clash in Mulberry Valley, Skye Fargo reported for the last time at Allan Pinkerton's office.

His eyes widened when America's most prominent detective, infamous for his frugality, slid a stack of double eagles across his desk to Fargo.

"A two-hundred-dollar bonus from the Pinkerton Agency," the Scottish sleuth announced. "And you and John will split the five-hundred-dollar reward from the U.S. Treasury as soon as Sarah and Burke are convicted in federal court. Write to me and I'll see that you get a bank draft."

Fargo grinned as he scooped up the shiny cartwheels. Half of it was going to Septimus to make up the full value of the horse Doyle had killed. The old liveryman had proved a stalwart friend, and Fargo didn't want to leave Saint Joe without settling that account.

"By the way," Pinkerton said, "did you see the story about Mayor Reece in this morning's paper?"

As if on cue, all three men laughed. The mystery of Josiah Reece's luxurious lifestyle had been exposed: The erstwhile politico, who spoke in glowing terms of "home and hearth," was the no-longer-secret owner of Cooter Brown's Grog Shop on notorious River Street—rumored to be the most profitable cathouse in Saint Joseph.

"So you're sticking it out with Allan?" Fargo said to Fowler.

The former constable shrugged. "Money in my pocket. There'll soon be plenty of work east of the Mississippi, Skye. You've heard that the Southern rebels have fired on Fort Sumter?"

Fargo nodded. "Bad medicine. I'm dusting my hocks west. It's gonna be a hell-buster back in the States."

"A national tragedy," Pinkerton agreed. "But what is bad for the nation is usually good for the Pinkerton Agency. The U.S. government is already clamoring for espionage agents."

"Throw in with me, Skye," Fowler urged. "We'll have great larks as spies. They're a big hit with the ladies."

"Spy Fargo," the Trailsman quipped. "It's got a nice ring to it, but I'd get fiddle-footed for purple sage and red rock canyons."

"You don't have to leave your beloved West to work for me," Pinkerton assured him. "War or no war, it looks certain that the Homestead Act will pass any day now. The Great

Plains will open to widespread settlement—civilization is coming with a bone in its teeth, Fargo, and it will inevitably overtake you. I'm opening more offices beyond the hundredth meridian—why not take a permanent job with one of them?"

"There's still the mountains and the desert. When they start fencing off Death Valley, maybe I'll look you up."

"Do," Pinkerton said with deep sincerity. "I had grave reservations when I first hired you. But now I understand why the newspaper wags declare you 'a man whom bees will not sting.' It's been an honor to know you, Skye Fargo."

Fargo's strong white teeth flashed through his beard. "Does this mean I'm spoken fo—?"

"Get out!" Pinkerton cut him off, grinning wide as he hooked a thumb toward the door.

Before Fargo returned to the livery to square with Septimus and rig the Ovaro for the trail, he made one more stop: the city jail.

"All right if I say adios to your female prisoner, Sheriff?" he asked Harney Winslowe.

"Yeah, but make sure you just *say* it," Winslowe grumped.

"I'll keep every part of my anatomy on this side of the bars," Fargo promised, heading down a narrow corridor leading to three small cells, only one of which was occupied. Sarah Hopewell sat before a small deal table, enjoying a steak with all the trimmings.

Fargo laughed. "Is this your last meal?"

"Hardly," she said primly. "The usual fare for prisoners is beans and hardtack. And I ordered strawberries and cream for breakfast. You see, the sheriff *likes* me."

Fargo shook his head in amazement. "Don't they all?"

She looked pretty and proper in a paisley shawl and a dress of Swiss muslin with a lace flounce on the skirt. "I hear you're leaving town?"

"Yep. I've just been hired as a hunter for a mapping expedition into the Bitterroot Range."

"Just had to stop by and gloat, right? Well, I hope a grizzly bear eats you."

"I wish you the best, too."

She set her fork down and dabbed at her lips with a linen napkin. Those gemlike blue eyes suddenly sparked with pent-up feeling. "Skye?"

"Mmm?"

"Didn't you *ever* fall for me? I mean, before you realized what a she-devil I am?"

Again Fargo shook his head in amazement. "Lady, you're the world-beatingest calico I ever knew. Here you are, headed off to court, then prison, and the only damn thing in that beautiful head of yours is worrying about the one man you couldn't snake charm?"

"Yes," she snapped petulantly. "That *is* on my mind night and day. I think you're a big, handsome liar! You *did* fall in love with me, just like all the others! Admit it!"

"Sorry. I'm in love with women, not woman. If it's any consolation, I do rate you mighty high for looks and brains. But you did one thing that's beyond pardon—you ordered the death of a woman. That won't go on the frontier."

"I *am* a woman, damn you!"

"Obviously, and that just makes it worse in my books."

"The noble code of the West, I suppose?"

"You suppose right. There's a lot of leeway on the frontier, plenty of crimes that can be overlooked. But not what you did."

She made a fist and struck the table, her pretty face twisting into a mask of fury. "She was a whore, you hypocrite! A filthy, low creature who let pigs like Jack Parsons rut on her! My God, Skye, she beat naked men with whips!"

"Whores are in it for money, Goldilocks. She might've been a mite strange, but what she did was done for fun. To chew it fine, *you're* the whore. You made a whore of your soul. I'll have a hundred more beautiful women while you're locked up in a penitentiary touching yourself under the blankets. You'll grow old and bitter and horse-faced, and one day your naked beauty will fade from my memory. But I'll remember Lily Reece until the day I die—and honor her memory."

His blunt, unexpected words shocked her to her core. Fargo touched the brim of his hat and turned to leave.

"You cruel bastard!" she cried out behind him. "You didn't come to say good-bye, did you? You came to deliberately twist the dagger in my heart!"

"The way you say," Fargo admitted without turning around. "Enjoy your steak . . . woman killer."

LOOKING FORWARD!
The following is the opening section of the next novel in the exciting *Trailsman* series from Signet:

TRAILSMAN #373
UTAH TERROR

The remote and rugged mountains of Utah Territory, 1861—where a hatchet in the back was a common way to die.

The mountains were green and lush with life, and deadly to man and beast alike.

Skye Fargo caught sight of a careless buck in a thicket. The buck heard the clomp of the Ovaro's hooves and raised its head for a look and ducked down again.

Drawing rein, Fargo sat as still as a statue with his Henry pressed to his shoulder and his cheek to the smooth brass, waiting for the buck to stick its head up again. He hadn't had a good meal in a week. The prospect of a thick venison steak made his mouth water.

The buck wasn't making the same mistake twice.

Fargo tried a trick. He whistled as high and as loud as he could, and the curious buck rose up for another look. "Got you," Fargo said to himself, and stroked the trigger.

"I can taste the meat already," Fargo said as he shoved the Henry into the saddle scabbard. He was talking to himself a lot of late. Alighting, he led the Ovaro to the thicket.

Retrieving the buck took effort. The bushes were so close together that it was a wonder the buck had wormed its way in. But bucks were good at hiding. He once saw a hunter walk right past one lying in tall grass and not notice it.

After a lot of pulling and grunting, Fargo got this one out of the thicket. Drawing his Arkansas toothpick from its ankle sheath, he set to work.

Most men would use a skinning knife or a bowie but he was partial to the toothpick. Double-edged, and sharp as a razor, it was light and slender enough that he could whip it out quickly if he had to.

Fargo didn't bother with fancy carving. He had no intention of saving and curing the hide; it was the meat he wanted. He impaled a hunk of haunch on a spit, kindled a fire, and sat watching the meat cook. His stomach rumbled and the aroma about made him want to bite into the meat raw.

It was as he was squatting there, his forearms across his knees, that the undergrowth crackled.

Instantly Fargo was erect with his hand on his Colt. A tall man, broad at the shoulders, he wore buckskins and boots and a white hat and red bandana. All had seen a lot of use.

Out of the woods came three men. To say Fargo was surprised was putting it mildly. For one thing, he wasn't aware of a town or settlement nearby. For another, the three were Chinese.

One was short and thin and had a weasel face that Fargo took a dislike to on sight. The man wore the usual Chinese garb and a small hat that made Fargo think of an upside down food bowl. The man stopped and whispered something to his companions.

The other two were squat and thick and wore matching black clothes. They listened and gave slight bobs of their heads. Both stuck their hands up their baggy sleeves and crossed their arms across their chests as they followed the weasel over.

"So sorry, sir," the weasel said, "for disturbing you at your meal."

"What do you want?" Fargo demanded. He had nothing against the Chinese. He didn't hate them as many whites did simply because they weren't white. But strangers too often spelled trouble, Chinese or otherwise.

"I am Lo Ping." The man gestured at the pair in black. "My associates are the Hu brothers."

"Good for you." Fargo was so hungry, his gut hurt. He wanted them to leave so he could get to eating.

Lo Ping smiled but it didn't touch his eyes. "We wonder if you have perhaps seen anyone in the past hour or so? We seek a girl who ran away from Hunan."

"Hunan?" Fargo repeated. "Who or what is that?"

"It is a gold camp, good sir," Lo Ping said. "Named after a province in China from which many of us at the camp are from."

"A gold camp this far out?" Fargo recollected that the last outpost he'd come across was fifty miles back.

Lo Ping nodded. "It is a new one. Run by Chinese, for Chinese."

"That's a first," Fargo said. He'd been to camps where Chinese made up part of the population but never to one exclusively so.

"About the girl," Lo Ping said. "Have you seen her, perhaps?"

"All I've seen is him," Fargo answered, with a nod at the buck. "And you."

"Ah." Lo Ping frowned. "Again, I am sorry to have disturbed you. We will depart." He started to turn but stopped. "If you should see her, and if you would bring her to Hunan, there will be a suitable reward."

"What is she? An outlaw?" Fargo joked.

"As I told you, she is a runaway," Lo Ping said. "She is most temperamental and does not like to do as she is told."

"Who does?" Fargo said.

"She dishonors her ancestors with her behavior," Lo Ping elaborated, with a hint of anger. "She has been paid for, and should accept her fate as everyone else does. We all have our purpose."

"I doubt I'll see her," Fargo said. "As soon as I'm done eating, I'll be on my way."

"That is good, sir," Lo Ping said.

Something in the man's tone rankled, a suggestion that Fargo was unwelcome. He tested his hunch by asking, "Is there a general store in this gold camp of yours? I could stand to buy some supplies."

Lo Ping frowned. "There is, but it does not carry much you can use."

"How the hell would you know?"

"It caters to Chinese needs," Lo Ping said. "Trust me when I say it would be wiser for you to buy your supplies elsewhere." He smiled and bobbed his head and walked off.

Moving as one, the Hu brothers turned and trailed after him.

Fargo shook his head in amusement. He didn't really need supplies and didn't give a damn about their gold camp. As soon as he finished eating, he'd move on.

Sinking back down, he breathed deep of the delicious aroma, and practically drooled. He was nothing if not patient, and he waited until the meat was cooked clear through before he removed the spit from the fire. He didn't bother taking it off the stick. Holding an end in either hand, he tore into the juicy venison with relish.

He liked beef more and buffalo best but deer meat was delicious in its own right. Closing his eyes, he chewed with the eagerness of a starved wolf.

When he opened his eyes, a girl was there.

She'd stepped from behind a tall spruce and stood eyeing him uncertainly. To call her a "girl" wasn't quite fitting; she was in her twenties, he reckoned, and her womanly attributes were enough to draw a man's eye despite her loose-fitting clothes. She wasn't wearing a dress. She had on a Chinese-style shirt and pants similar to those the three men had worn, and sandals. Her black hair was cropped at the shoulders. Her eyes were a penetrating brown, her full lips inviting.

Fargo stopped chewing and said with his mouth full, "Well, now."

She gnawed her lower lip and gazed nervously in the direction Lo Ping and the Hu brothers had gone.

"Who might you be?" Fargo asked.

She stared at him.

"Do you speak English?"

All she did was stare.

"Are you hungry?" Fargo said, motioning at the buck. "I have plenty to spare." He waited but when all she did was continue to stare, he shrugged and took another bite.

The girl inched closer. She seemed undecided if she could trust him.

On an impulse Fargo cut off a piece and held it out to her. "Here."

She stopped and did more staring.

"You're damn ridiculous," Fargo said, and tossed the piece at her feet.

Warily, almost timidly, she tucked at the knees and carefully plucked the meat from the ground. She sniffed it a few times, then brushed it off and tried a tiny bite. Evidently she wasn't used to eating deer. She swallowed, and smiled, and bit off a bigger mouthful.

"That's more like it," Fargo said. He indicated a spot across the fire. "You're welcome to join me if you'd like."

She understood. She eased down cross-legged and regarded him with what he took to be more than casual interest.

"Skye Fargo," he introduced himself, and tapped his chest. He pointed at her. "What's your name?"

She didn't respond.

"Name," Fargo said. He tapped his chest again. "Fargo." He pointed at her and arched his brows.

She took another bite of venison.

"Oh, well." Fargo shrugged. He hadn't had many dealings with the Chinese, and while he spoke Spanish and could hold up his end of a conversation in half a dozen Indian tongues, he didn't know a lick of her language.

She finished and wiped her fingers on the grass. "May I please have another piece, kind sir? It is very good and I am starved."

Fargo glanced up. "So you do know English?" He took the toothpick from his lap. "You can have as much as you'd like." He cut off a larger chunk and tossed it across the fire.

She deftly snatched it out of the air. "Thank you very much. It has been two days since I ate last."

"You're the one those gents were after," Fargo said. "The girl who ran away from the gold camp."

"Did they tell you why?"

"Something about you don't like being told what to do," Fargo recollected.

"There is more to it than that," she said. "I refuse to let a man touch me if I do not want him to."

Fargo thought he savvied. "Does Lo Ping want to get in those pants of yours?"

"Get in my—?" she said, and her cheeks became pink. "Oh. No. It is not like that. I would not have him for my man if he were the last man on earth."

Fargo laughed.

"I refuse to work for Madame Lotus and ran away. Han sent Lo Ping and his hatchet men after me."

"Hatchet men?" Fargo said.

"Yes. They—" She looked past him, and stiffened and pushed to her feet.

Fargo suspected what he would see before he turned.

Lo Ping and the Hu brothers were back. Lo Ping smiled his oily smile and crooked a finger at the girl. "We have found you. You will come along and not cause trouble."

"I will not," the girl declared.

"You have no choice."

Fargo couldn't say what made him do what he did next. Maybe it was how Lo Ping made his skin crawl. Maybe he didn't like to see the girl bullied. Or maybe he was just pissed that they kept interrupting his meal. Whatever his reason, he stood and faced them and said, "Sure she does."

Lo Ping scowled. "This is not your concern. Leave her to us and go about your business."

"And if I don't?" Fargo said.

"You will be taught a lesson in manners," Lo Ping warned. "And it will not be pleasant."